DEMON Chick

DEMON Chick

MARILYN KAYE

Henry Holt
and Company
NEW YORK

Henry Holt and Company, LLC
Publishers since 1866
175 Fifth Avenue
New York, New York 10010
www.HenryHoltKids.com

Library of Congress Cataloging-in-Publication Data
Kaye, Marilyn.
Demon chick / Marilyn Kaye.—1st ed.
p.   cm.
Summary: Sixteen-year-old Jessica discovers that her mother, a charismatic presidential
candidate, sold Jessica's soul to the devil in exchange for political power.
ISBN-13: 978-0-8050-8880-9 / ISBN-10: 0-8050-8880-6
[1. Mothers and daughters—Fiction.   2. Hell—Fiction.   3. Politics, Practical—Fiction.]   I. Title.
PZ7.K2127De 2009   [Fic]—dc22   2008050280

First Edition—2009 / Designed by April Ward
Printed in the United States of America on acid-free paper. ∞
1   3   5   7   9   10   8   6   4   2

*For Dyan Sheldon, who loved this story, and for
Penny Holroyde, who made me write it*

DEMON CHICK

chapter One

ATEACHER ONCE told my creative-writing class that every good story has a beginning, a middle, and an end. Well, *duh*.

But once I'd made up my mind to write this particular story, I realized that the rule might not be so simple to follow. Naturally, I wanted to tell *my* story from *my* point of view, so I couldn't really start at the beginning, because I wasn't around when it all began, I wasn't even born yet. So I decided to kick off my tale at the point when I first realized that my life was interesting enough to make a story. Or maybe just before it got to be interesting, so I could set the stage and create some suspense. (I wasn't really worried that readers might guess what was about to happen. If you've been leading a relatively normal life, if you've never been exposed to the darker side of the human spirit or vacationed in the bottomless pits of Hell, this should all be pretty new to you.) So, to begin my story, I chose the morning of the day before my life first started to become story-worthy.

I was sitting on the broad stone steps leading up to the residence hall at six-forty-five on a Saturday morning in late October, a day that happened to be my sixteenth birthday. The car wasn't supposed to pick me up until seven, but I'd come down from my room early so I could jump right in and take off the second it arrived. There was a very real possibility that the vehicle would be a long black stretch limo, with a uniformed chauffeur and maybe even bodyguards, and I didn't want them hanging around and waiting in front of the dorm for everyone to see.

I don't know why I cared—limos had been seen around here before. Woodbridge wasn't the ritziest girls' boarding school in Virginia, but it had its fair share of potential kidnap victims. There were at least half a dozen offspring of government big shots, plus the daughter of the ambassador of some fabulously rich oil country. Not to mention the daughter of a movie legend, a Mafia princess, a real princess, the twin daughters of a Greek shipping tycoon, and two sisters who called an aging rock star Daddy. In fact, up until very recently, on the rich-and-famous food chain I was definitely a bottom feeder. So no one at Woodbridge would gape at the sight of a limo, no one would care if it was me getting into it, and besides, at this hour on a Saturday morning, everyone was sleeping.

But no, not everyone. A slender girl wearing shorts and a sweat-stained T-shirt appeared from around the side of the building. She was jogging slowly, clearly at the end of her run, and when she reached the front of the dorm, she stopped. Placing one foot up on the third step, she greeted me as she began stretching.

"Hi, Jessica."

"Hey, Kip."

Kip Simmonds lived on my hall, just a few rooms down from mine. I had no idea what Kip was short for. She shifted legs and noticed my suitcase.

"Going away?"

"Home," I replied. "For the weekend." Her eyebrows

were still up in questioning mode, and she'd taken the iPod 'phones out of her ears, so I felt obliged to offer more information. "It's my birthday."

She nodded. "Oh. Happy birthday."

"Thanks."

She was okay, Kip. I didn't know her all that well—actually, I didn't know anyone at Woodbridge all that well—but she was one of the few I'd had mini-conversations with (mostly along the lines of "How did you do on the algebra quiz?" "I choked." "Yeah, me, too"). She wasn't a friend, exactly, but she was friendly, and she never made any cracks about my mother. Right now, she seemed to be trying to find something more to say or ask so she wouldn't be cutting off the conversation too quickly.

"Is it far?"

"Huh?"

"Your home. Is it far from here?"

Having never traveled from Woodbridge to this particular "home," I wasn't sure, but I could hazard a guess. "Less than three hours. Near Leesburg."

"Oh, up north. That will be pretty. The leaves should be turning by now."

I tried to work up some show of enthusiasm. "Yeah, maybe. Hope so." I couldn't think of anything else to say on the topic of autumn foliage, and she must have decided she'd been sufficiently sociable.

"Well, have a nice weekend. See ya."

"See ya," I echoed as she ran up the stairs. Even though she was a perfectly okay person, I was relieved to see her leave. It wasn't easy for me to make casual conversation with classmates. Most Woodbridge girls in my year had been together for two full years now. I'd just transferred five weeks ago, and I'd been keeping a low profile, which hadn't been that difficult. I was a loner by nature, and pretty much content to hang out in my single room with my books and my PC.

I didn't participate in any activities, either, which was probably why I didn't recognize the two boys I now observed coming up the circular driveway. They were both looking around in a suspiciously furtive way, and when one of them spotted me, he grabbed the other guy's arm and nodded in my direction. They stopped, put their heads together, nodded in what looked like agreement, and then continued in the direction of the residence hall.

I wasn't alarmed. There were two boys' schools in the vicinity, Buford and St. Something, and the single-sex schools tried to keep hormones from raging out of control by holding regular joint events—drama clubs, dances, that sort of thing. Rules were posted in student handbooks about visiting outside the scheduled events, but I knew there were girls who sneaked out and boys who sneaked in at other times. In all likelihood, at that very moment there were a couple of girls waiting at a security exit for these two.

Trying not to be obvious, I gave them the once-over as they drew closer. Juniors, maybe seniors, I figured. The skinny dark one had on those oversized jeans hanging from below his hips, and for the zillionth time I wondered how they keep those pants up. The other one wore regular jeans with a sleeveless sweatshirt that exposed nice tanned arms. But it was his face that really drew me—he was boy-band handsome, with I-just-woke-up shaggy blond hair falling into eyes so blue I could identify the color while he was still yards away. Normally, I wasn't attracted to pretty boys, but I would have made an exception for this one if I ever had the opportunity. Of course, the probability factor of that hovered just around null.

4

Eye contact was unavoidable, and the skinny one grunted in greeting. Pretty Boy actually spoke.

"Hey."

"Hey," I replied.

They were studying the big glass-enclosed bulletin board on a pedestal by the stairs. Now that we'd all acknowledged each other's presence, I felt entitled to watch as the blond took a screwdriver out of his backpack and began working on the nails that held the glass to the board. In the process, he glanced at me with raised eyebrows. I nodded to assure him I had no intention of protesting or reporting his clearly unauthorized use of the official-news-only board. Meanwhile, the other one unrolled a poster.

Once the plate of glass was off, the skinny guy covered the school announcements with the poster, and the blond secured it with Scotch tape. I leaned forward to look at the poster and read it silently.

THOU SHALT NOT KILL.
RALLY IN SUPPORT OF ALTON CRENSHAW.
SATURDAY, 2 P.M., GREAT LAWN, ST. ANDREWS.

While the blond replaced the glass, the other one caught my eye.

"You know who Alton Crenshaw is?" he asked.

His skeptical tone annoyed me, so I had to respond with something beyond a simple "yes."

"He's scheduled to be executed by lethal injection on Wednesday for the murder of a family in Richmond fifteen years ago. Some people say he might be retarded."

"Mentally challenged," the blond said, but with a grin that mocked his own effort at political correctness.

I smiled back and continued with my efforts to impress him. "A psychologist for the defense testified that his IQ was way below average, but the prosecution presented tests that said he's normal."

He nodded with what I hoped was approval. "And it doesn't matter anyway," he said, "because capital punishment is just plain wrong, even if the killer's a genius. It's cruel and unusual punishment."

"Right," I said, with a conviction that belied the gazillions of high-school debates on the subject. "Anyway, the Supreme Court turned down his final appeal yesterday."

"Very good," he said, making his approval clear this time. "So—are you going to tell all your friends and come to the rally?"

At that very moment, a car turned off the main road, and Skinny grabbed Blondie's arm. "Yo, Sanders, let's get out of here."

"Don't be stupid. Security doesn't drive Lincoln Town Cars."

Apparently, someone on my mother's staff had taste. The car that pulled up in front of us was clearly expensive, but it wasn't a limousine, and the man who got out of the driver's seat wasn't wearing a gold-braided uniform, just a simple dark suit.

"Miss Hunsucker?"

Nodding, I rose, and the driver took my suitcase. I didn't look at the boys, but I could hear a swift intake of breath coming from one of them. It was getting very hard to maintain a low profile with a name like Hunsucker. As I got into the back seat of the car, I debated turning to offer the cute guy some sort of parting smile, but I knew what I'd see on his face—disbelief, maybe disgust. I'd been seeing a lot of that lately, and I was getting used to it, but to see it on such a gorgeous face—it would be way too depressing.

In any case, the driver had already closed the door, so there was no point in smiling for his benefit—the windows of the car were made of that smoky stuff so people on the outside couldn't see in. Besides, if I looked at him, I'd have to suffer the memory of his expression, and he wouldn't even see my apologetic smile. Which was all I had to offer.

"Would you like some music, Miss Hunsucker?" the chauffeur asked.

"Uh, no thanks," I said. Then, to make it clear that I didn't consider myself to be so much more important than he was, I added, "But if *you* want music, it's fine with me."

"No, thank you, ma'am."

Ma'am. I was barely sixteen years old, for crying out loud. I wasn't entitled to that kind of respect.

I leaned back in the very comfortable seat and tried not to think about the boys—the *boy*—I'd just left behind. Sanders— that was what the other guy had called him. First or last name? I'd noticed that some guys called one another by their last names, but a lot of high-class kids around here had first names that sounded like last names. Of course, the really significant name was mine—and, given Sanders's mission to protest capital punishment, he must have had a pretty negative reaction to it. But why did this bother me so much? I didn't even know him.

Dumb question. I was bothered because he was so cute, so hot; I was attracted to him on a totally shallow and superficial level. Which was okay, because I was sixteen, and if I didn't deserve respect I was entitled to be at least *occasionally* shallow.

On the other hand, I doubted that the attraction would

have been mutual, no matter what my last name was. I wasn't his type. Guys like that went with girls who equaled or surpassed them in the looks department. He was out of my league.

I wasn't ugly. There just wasn't anything particularly outstanding about the way I looked. I could have been the poster child for "ordinary teenage girl"—average height, average weight. Braces on my teeth. Glasses, under which one could barely make out plain brown eyes. Brown hair—straight and falling just below my shoulders in no style whatsoever. Ears, nose, mouth—yes, I had them all, and there was nothing remarkable about any of them. Nobody would look at me on the street and think "ugly"—no one would even *look*.

Which was really okay by me. At this point in my life, I didn't crave attention. But I knew it was going to get harder and harder to avoid.

From my shoulder bag, I pulled out the magazine I'd bought yesterday. I had gone into town to get it, even though I could have bought it right here on campus, in the school store. It just wasn't something I wanted to be seen buying or carrying.

I had no difficulty identifying the woman on the cover as my mother. The likeness was good enough, and the photographer had captured Margaret Hunsucker in a pose familiar to anyone who'd seen her before, even if it was just on TV. There was the usual direct gaze of the pale-blue eyes, the thin lips that suggested just the faintest hint of a smile, the slight thrust of the chin. I thought there might have been a little airbrushing—her complexion looked awfully smooth, with a delicate peachy-pink flush on the cheeks, and her dark-blond hair was immaculately coiffed. But even with the touch-ups, she was immediately recognizable, so much so that the magazine's editor hadn't bothered to put a name with the face. The only words on the cover formed a question: "Is this the face of the first female president of the United States?"

I opened the magazine to the cover story and started to read.

More rumors than pigeons were flying over Capitol Hill last week. Could it be true? Can a third-party candidate present a real challenge to the Democratic and Republican nominees? And is America ready for a woman as president?

The question appears to have become rhetorical, since the answer is clearly a resounding yes. Senator Hunsucker's popularity within her own up-and-coming party, and her appeal, which has begun to cross party lines, have pushed her into real contention to be leader of the free world.

But although she has been in the public eye for almost twenty years, there are still voters who are now wondering, just who *is* Margaret Hunsucker?

Good question, I thought, and I was glad no one was asking *me*. I didn't expect the article to provide any real insight, and as I read it, my expectations were met. Maybe I didn't know my mother well, but there wasn't much here that I didn't already know.

Born Margaret Tribble in 1967 in a rural Southern commune to a couple of young high-school dropouts. Raised in an "alternative" life style, which apparently didn't suit her, since much of her political philosophy rested on concepts of traditional family standards and values. Left school and home at the age of sixteen, moved to the capital of a certain state in the Southeastern region of the United States. Picked up secretarial skills, found a civil-service job typing. Got noticed by the seventy-three-year-old lieutenant governor of the state, Harley Hunsucker, and married him when she was twenty-one.

What I knew about *him* was that he must have been a very popular guy, since during his lifetime he held just about every elected position available in the state. From what I'd read, he started off as a mayor in some bum-fuck nowhere town, and then became a representative for the region in the state government. From there it was just a hop, skip, and jump to the U.S. House of Representatives, which was followed by a two-term gig as governor. That was when he made the name that gave him legendary status, through a photograph any American kid would recognize from any ninth-grade history textbook.

It was reprinted here, and I'd seen it before, but I adjusted my glasses and examined the photo more closely. There he was, in glorious black and white, with his stomach protruding over his belt, a smug grin on his jowly face, and his arms folded across his chest. He stood on the top of some steps, blocking the entrance to a high school. At the bottom of the steps stood half a dozen black teenagers, their faces reflecting a range of feelings from disappointment to confusion to anger.

The photographer who took it won some kind of big journalism prize. Now the photo is considered to be a classic illustration of the civil-rights struggle, with dear old Dad as a symbol of segregation and racism.

If you managed to stay awake in your ninth-grade history class, you'll know that Presidents Kennedy and Johnson and the Civil Rights Act of 1964 pushed him off those steps, but that wasn't the end of Harley Hunsucker. Unbelievable as it may seem, he still had his followers, lots of them, and they petitioned to change the law so he could run for governor a third time. When they couldn't pull that off, they elected him to the U.S. Senate, where he could sit forever. He stayed there until he was in his early seventies, when he began saying incredibly stupid things that got picked up by C-SPAN and CNN. At that point, his political cronies got together and figured out a way to stop him from embarrassing the state, and to salvage his pride. They got him on the next ballot for lieutenant governor, a position that, in this state, essentially consisted of going to funerals that the governor was too busy to attend.

That was when he met my mother.

He'd been married before—in fact, his first wife had died during his last year in the Senate. They'd never had any children, and though I'm sure there was a lot of talk about him marrying such a young woman, I think his pals were just happy to know he wouldn't be alone in his declining years.

When he was no longer physically able to perform his duties, his young wife took over the largely ceremonial functions of his office. And when he died, the party put her on the ballot to replace him. She won.

But her role as high-school graduation speaker and ribbon cutter was soon to change. Quick to learn the ins and outs of government workings, and endowed with a remarkably charismatic appeal, Lieutenant Governor Margaret Hunsucker became the most popular person in the state administration. And when the party didn't nominate her for governor in the next election, her supporters formed a new party, and for the first time in history a write-in candidate was elected governor.

I remembered this. I was only five, but I could recall the flashes of light as cameras snapped me, and I could still see my new pink room in the governor's mansion. And I remembered the nannies—first Mary Alice, then Louise, and after

Louise there was Denise . . . no, Jenny, and Denise after her. And a couple of others whose names had faded away. Why so many? Had I been some sort of rotten kid? Or had Margaret Hunsucker been a horrible employer?

None of the nannies stayed long enough for me to form a real attachment to any of them. In fact, I couldn't remember ever feeling connected to anyone. Certainly not my mother—I rarely saw her. And there were no real friends, either. I was taken by chauffeur to my private school every morning, and picked up there in the afternoon. I was never invited to other kids' homes—or maybe I was, but I was never permitted to go. And I certainly hadn't been encouraged to invite anyone back to the mansion.

I must have been a lonely child, though I don't recall being unhappy. I had lots of toys, games, and books, and I guess I just learned to enjoy solitary pleasures. Things changed a little when I turned twelve and Governor Hunsucker became Senator Hunsucker. She moved to the Washington, D.C., area, and I was shipped off to Hillside, a boarding school up east. By then, I'd become such a loner by nature, it wasn't easy to form relationships and socialize. Eventually, I made a couple of friends, and after a few years I was actually comfortable at Hillside. But then Senator Hunsucker started to think about becoming President Hunsucker, and she wanted me closer—not *too* close, just close enough to be summoned at a moment's notice for photo ops. Besides, a politician who promoted family values had to demonstrate some evidence of a family.

The article didn't say much about me—just a note that I'd been born three months after the death of Harley Hunsucker. There was a picture, but I couldn't even recognize myself. It must have been taken at my mother's inauguration as governor. I was cowering behind the nanny-of-the-moment, thumb in mouth, and glasses already hiding part of my face. Margaret Hunsucker, hand on Bible, faced a black-robed man.

A mild wave of nausea or something like that passed over me. I wasn't sure why—she'd never mistreated me or anything like that. We didn't fight; in fact, I couldn't recall a single conversation that had encompassed any subject beyond the weather and my general state of health. There was a time, a couple of years ago, when I was ordered out of my jeans and into a skirt for a photo, but that wasn't enough reason to hate her. I wasn't crazy about her politics, but that wasn't the reason, either. I wasn't even sure I *did* hate her. Maybe she frightened me. To be perfectly honest, I couldn't come up with a reason to feel any kind of intense hostility toward her. True, she hadn't given me much motherly time, but that had to be the same for any woman in her position. I should probably cut her some slack. Like I said, I didn't even *know* her, not really.

So maybe I should do something about that. This could be the weekend to get closer, to make some sort of connection. If I insisted that I wanted some time to talk, surely she wouldn't refuse me, not on my birthday. I could find out more about her politics, her platform. Even if we disagreed on stuff like capital punishment, we could discuss it, we could have a lively debate. She might be feeling just as uncomfortable with our relationship as I did. Maybe she felt nauseated when she thought about *me*. It was time to do something about this, I decided, and even though the thought of talking to her made me nervous, it also gave me a sensation I'd never before associated with going to see her—mild optimism.

By the time we reached the big gray house on the hill, I was almost cheerful.

"You're home, Miss Hunsucker," the driver announced as he turned into the long, winding uphill driveway. The man in the little guardhouse peered inside the car, gave the driver the thumbs-up, and opened the gate.

Home. What a strange word to apply to this place. I'd been there before, but never for periods long enough to dignify it with that word.

It was the only house on the hill, and surrounded by enough trees to practically constitute a forest, but its seclusion didn't make it quiet. The parking area in back of the house was chaotic, with people running in and out. There were vans labeled with the names of TV stations and newspapers. When the driver opened my door, cameras flashed and clicked, so I ducked my head, but I didn't think anyone was paying attention to me. Margaret Hunsucker had just emerged from the back door.

A petite young woman with short curly blond hair preceded her, and made sweeping motions with her arms to create an opening in the crowd that had immediately surrounded my mother. Margaret Hunsucker strode forward, and I had barely enough time to catch a glimpse of her face before she gathered me into her arms. I froze, from complete shock. Hugging had never been a Hunsucker family tradition.

Camera lights flashed. Then she held me at arm's length. "Jessica, darling, I'm so sorry to have to run off like this, but I can't get out of this meeting. I know you understand." She was speaking pretty loudly, and I could see reporters jotting down her words.

"But you're going to have a wonderful day with Lisa, and tonight we'll celebrate your birthday in grand style!"

"Who's Lisa?" I asked, but by now my mother had been hauled away by men in dark sunglasses and placed in a limousine. The young short-haired woman was now taking my arm.

"Jessica, hi, I'm Lisa, your mother's aide. And just wait till you hear what's been planned for you today!"

"What?"

"A makeover! Oh, we are going to have so much fun! Let's go, there's no time to lose."

I wasn't even given the opportunity to follow my suitcase to my bedroom or use a bathroom. She dragged me over to a cute little sports car. "And it's just you and me, no bodyguards, no chauffeurs. Isn't that fabulous?"

Clearly, she didn't expect a response, and I wouldn't have known what to say anyway. I'd never seen this woman before in my life. How should I know if it was going to be fabulous, spending a day together?

As a natural cynic, I had a pretty good idea what this makeover was all about. With the presidential campaign, I was bound to be in the public eye, and my mother wanted me to look good. But I couldn't really say I minded. I could definitely use a haircut, and, thinking about that boy with the poster back at school, I wasn't exactly averse to tweaking my appearance a little.

Lisa got into the driver's seat. "Ready?"

I fastened my seat belt, and we took off.

chapter
TWO

LISA TOOK her eyes from the road just long enough to flash me an enormous smile. "You must be so excited."

"I've never had a makeover before," I admitted.

She tossed back her head and laughed. "Actually, I was referring to the fact that your mother has a good chance of becoming the next president of the United States."

I felt like an idiot. "Oh, that, right. Yeah." I glanced at her curiously. "Do you really think she can win?"

"Of course she can win!" Lisa chirped. "And you're going to help her by looking fantastic."

I had doubts as to whether attractive offspring could have such an impact on voters, but I tried to show enthusiasm. "Do you think I should cut my bangs?"

She didn't look at me. "Mmm . . . well, here we are at our first stop!" She parked the car in front of a sober five-story brick office building that didn't look like the kind of place that would hold a salon or a spa. This was confirmed by the sign over the door: "Eastside Medical Center."

I felt a little unnerved, and made this clear. "I'm not having plastic surgery."

"Of course not," Lisa assured me. She offered nothing else by way of explanation. Holding the door of the building open, she ushered me in and then led me to an office on the first floor. The label on the door read "R. G. Pearson, M.D. Ophthalmology."

"What are we doing here?"

"You have to lose those glasses," Lisa said, and opened the door.

"But I've tried contacts before," I told her. "They make my eyes itch. Besides, I've already got an eye doctor."

Either Lisa hadn't heard me or she was intentionally ignoring me. In any case, she was halfway through the door before I'd finished expressing my objection. Feeling somewhat like an obedient puppy, I followed her.

"We have an appointment with Dr. Pearson for corrective laser surgery," Lisa told the woman at the reception desk. "The name is Madeline Curtis."

I didn't know which was more startling—the word "surgery" or the name that wasn't mine. As the receptionist directed us to the waiting area, I stared at Lisa in bewilderment. She patted my hand reassuringly. "It doesn't hurt at all, you know," she said. "I know lots of people who have had it done."

I'd heard of this kind of eye treatment, and I knew it was pretty common these days. But it was still surgery, and I was appalled that a decision like this could have been made without asking me. "But these are *my* eyes," I argued. "Don't you think I should have some say in this?"

Lisa looked slightly taken aback, but she recovered quickly. "Of course you should, Jessica. This was your mother's idea—she thought you'd appreciate being able to see without glasses. But if you *like* wearing glasses. . . ."

What could I say? Did anyone *like* wearing glasses? I'd just never given them any thought. On the other hand, since I had to take them off to read, I was always putting them down somewhere and losing them, and that was a pain. And I never had any cleaning cloths with me, so there was always a messy streak or two defacing everything I looked at. I imagined waking up in the morning and actually being able to see, instead of fumbling and knocking everything off my bedside table reaching for my glasses.

So I agreed to the surgery. I sat in a reclining chair, the doctor stuck some contraption on me to keep my eyes open, he put drops in my eyes and aimed streams of light at them. Lisa hadn't lied—it didn't hurt, and it took all of about five minutes. Afterward, I was given some thick sunglasses with cardboard frames and told that in a few hours I could take them off and see perfectly. It was totally no big deal. The only really weird thing was the fact that the doctor kept calling me Madeline.

"Why did I have to use a fake name?" I asked Lisa as we left.

"Oh, Jess, you've got a lot to learn about celebrity," Lisa told me, but the warmth in her tone took any censure out of the comment. "Do you think Britney Spears would make a doctor's appointment under her own name?"

"No, I guess not," I replied, and for the zillionth time I wished my family had a slightly less unusual name. With the drops in my eyes and the dark glasses, my vision was fuzzy, but I could make out the arrows by the elevator door. I reached for the "down" arrow, but Lisa was quicker and hit "up."

"Where now?" I asked. "Dermatology?" My skin wasn't bad at the moment, but I wouldn't have minded a fancy expensive potion to prevent future breakouts.

"You'll see," Lisa sang out as the elevator doors closed. When they opened, she led me directly across the hall. I couldn't make out the name or title on the door, but when Lisa opened it, an unmistakable odor of mint mouthwash hit me. "Dentist?"

"Orthodontist. Time to lose those chains on your teeth."

"You're kidding!" I cried out in delight. "I'm not supposed to get them off till January."

"Most orthodontists are way too old-fashioned when it comes to braces," Lisa informed me. "I've found a modern one."

But even this modern orthodontist had some reservations about taking my braces off three months early. "Your teeth are looking good, Monica," he said as he examined them. (I was Monica Cisco in this incarnation.) "But they could shift if we remove the apparatus too soon."

"I'll wear a retainer every night," I promised, but it was Lisa who found a better way to convince him.

"Monica's an actress," she told him, "and she's up for a big part. I'm her agent, and we're flying to the coast tomorrow for her screen test, and she won't have a chance if she's still wearing braces."

"But—"

"You don't want to be responsible for a young girl missing out on the opportunity of a lifetime, do you? And we'll return in just a few days to have the braces put back on."

"That's going to be very expensive," the orthodontist warned her, but Lisa brushed away that objection.

"Believe me, doctor, once she gets this film, money won't be an issue for Monica Cisco."

He looked at me doubtfully, and I couldn't blame him. But somehow Lisa had pulled it off. He slapped a gas mask over my nose—another surprise; I didn't think you could get laughing gas for something like this. I guess you can get anything you pay for. I floated off to my own version of the coast, La-La Land. When I came back to earth, he was holding a mirror in front of me.

Lisa had me out of the chair before I could fully admire

my metal-free mouth. Within seconds, she'd paid the orthodontist, assured him of our return the following week, and pushed me out the door.

"Good luck on your screen test, Miss Cisco" was still ringing in my ears when we got back into the car.

"Now for the fun stuff!" Lisa declared as she revved the engine. Still a little foggy from the nitrous oxide, I could only smile and nod and hope that the next step of the makeover would be something a little less invasive. I was relieved when we pulled into another strip mall and Lisa parked in front of Hair Today.

I tugged on a stringy lock that I wasn't terribly attached to, and thought about what I could do with it. I had to admit, I'd always had a fantasy of becoming a blonde, but I was pretty sure this wasn't on my mother's agenda. Which was why I laughed in the reception area of the salon when Lisa showed me a photo in a hairstyle magazine.

"What do you think of that?"

I studied the picture of an archetypal punk chick with a pink-and-green Statue of Liberty crown. "Perfect. That's a real Hunsucker hairdo."

"Shh," Lisa hissed. "No real names. Seriously, Jessica. It looks like fun."

I gazed at her askance. "You *do* work for my mother, right? Or are you some kind of spy trying to create friction in the organization?"

Lisa threw back her head and laughed uproariously. I didn't think my comment had been all *that* funny, but Lisa seemed barely able to stop giggling. "I know what you mean. Your mother's style is pretty conservative. But she made it very clear to me that you should feel free to be yourself."

I got it—this was some kind of psychological trick. She would offer something truly outrageous so I'd respond negatively and choose something very straight just to be disagreeable.

"I know, this look is pretty wild," Lisa continued. "But you could get away with it, I think."

I blinked. "You're kidding."

"No, I'm not. Jess . . . how well do you know your mother?"

This was the second or third time she'd called me Jess, and no one called me that, but I didn't tell her. I was too intrigued by her question. "Not well," I replied. "She was never around all that much when I was growing up."

"She realizes that," Lisa said, "and she has enormous regrets. With the campaign and, hopefully, her election, this situation won't change very much. She knows she can't make up for her negligence in the past, but at least she can try to improve your quality of life now."

Your quality of life. . . . It seemed like a political phrase to me. But in all fairness, I was impressed, and the thoughts I'd had on the ride from Woodbridge came back to me. Could I have misjudged Margaret Hunsucker all these years? Was it possible the woman actually had feelings for me? "She's not afraid I'll embarrass her?"

She shook her head. "She knows you wouldn't do anything intentionally to hurt her." She paused, and frowned. "You wouldn't, would you?"

I'd never considered the possibility—I wasn't that aggressive. I just basically wanted to be left alone. "No, of course not."

Lisa smiled. "Your mother doesn't want you to feel constricted by the nature of her constituency."

I elaborated on that last word: "Fascist meatheads."

Lisa looked pained. "That's an exaggeration, Jessica, and you know it. You're too intelligent to be so easily swayed by the liberal media."

I raised my eyebrows.

"Okay, okay," Lisa said hastily. "You're right, her constituency is pretty right-wing."

I was actually beginning to like Lisa, but I was still having a hard time buying her story. "And you're going to tell me that she isn't worried about what her voters think about her personal life, the way her daughter looks, stuff like that?"

"She says your happiness is more important to her," Lisa replied.

I didn't know what to say. I kept reminding myself that Lisa was in a public-relations position, which meant that she was a professionally trained liar and couldn't be believed. On the other hand, what purpose could it serve her to go against my mother? If I actually showed up this evening with pink and green spikes on my head, I might get some dirty looks, but who would really suffer? *Her* job was on the line here.

I looked at the photo again. I didn't really like it—punk had never appealed to me, and it would only draw more attention. But if something like this was acceptable. . . .

"How about blond?" I wondered. "And . . . short?"

Lisa beamed. "Excellent idea. Just between you and me, I thought this was a little extreme myself. I just wanted to show you the options."

I was liking her more and more. As my hair was being washed, I even began wondering if Lisa might prove to be a big help in getting closer to my mother. It had also begun to occur to me that perhaps Margaret Hunsucker was less narrow-minded than I'd always thought. Of course, she was representing an extreme right-wing party, but maybe she had plans to move it more toward the center. Or were the warm suds and this lovely head massage lulling me into an exaggerated sense of well-being?

I had plenty of time to daydream. The hairdresser seemed

to be cutting one hair at a time, and while Lisa hovered over her and gave instructions, I envisioned a future very different from the one I'd been anticipating. If my mother was really interested in the quality of my life, I could try to convince her that an all-girls boarding school wasn't the place for me. But where could I go instead?

I'd had a fantasy, for a long time. I frequently imagined myself in a foreign city, Paris or London or Rome, where I'd change my name and be the mysterious American painter or writer who lived alone in a garret. But with Secret Service people living next door? That was how it would have to be if my mother became president.

Peroxide fumes were stinging my eyes, so I closed them and considered another possibility. What if my mother was elected president and wanted me to live with her? She'd made such a big deal about the importance of families in all her campaigns (traditional families, of course, not single-parent or same-sex). And if she really wanted to make up for all those years of neglect, this would make sense. Was that what was in store for me? Little White House on the Prairie?

I tried to think of other presidential daughters. Chelsea Clinton had been younger than me, so of course she'd lived with her parents at the White House. The Bush twins were older than me, so they'd been away at universities. Of course, if I lived in the White House, there'd be no way to hide my identity. But it could be interesting. . . .

My reverie was interrupted by the hairdresser's cry of "Ta-da!" I opened my eyes and faced my new reflection.

I was stunned. I'd watched makeover programs on TV, but usually they involved all kinds of plastic surgery and weight loss, so I could understand the shock of the participants. I had no idea a change in hairstyle could make such a big difference in a person.

"What do you think?" the stylist asked anxiously.

I was still trying to identify this girl who was looking back at me, and I took off my laser-surgery shades. The eyes were bigger, the teeth were straight and gleaming white, and the short, practically platinum blond hair had been gelled and styled in a way I'd only seen on models in magazines. It gave my face a different shape—I even had cheekbones! And for the first time ever in my entire life, I thought I looked *hot*.

Behind me, Lisa was smiling broadly. "You love it, I can tell."

"I do," I whispered. "I really, really do. I still can't believe it's me."

"It's you, Marla," the stylist said happily.

"Why do all my fake names begin with M?" I asked Lisa as we left the salon.

"It was the only way I could remember them all," Lisa replied. "Your mother signs everything M, and it's carved on my brain."

"What's it like, working for her?" I asked, with real curiosity.

Lisa didn't take time to ponder the question, and when she replied, there was no hesitancy. "Your mother is brilliant. Her ideas are absolutely amazing. I'm just thrilled to be connected with her."

She spoke with a fervor that was almost religious. It gave me a little chill. "Really?"

"Yes." Lisa looked at her watch. "We've got an hour before your appointment with the makeup artist." She looked down the row of shops in the strip mall. "Want a suntan?"

"Isn't that supposed to give you skin cancer?" I asked uncertainly. Then I spotted something more interesting among the shops. "How about a tattoo?"

Lisa looked thoughtful. This couldn't have been part of her assignment, and I could tell it was going to be a real test of my mother's new attitude toward my appearance. "Nothing too radical," I assured her. "No skulls. A flower, maybe. Or a heart."

Lisa nodded. "Sure. Why not?"

I ended up with a butterfly on my right shoulder. It hurt like unbelievable, so when the guy finished I decided I might as well go with the pain and get some piercings. This time I was completely floored when Lisa agreed to an eyebrow hoop and a crystal on my left nostril. The tattoo could always be hidden with sleeves—but the jewelry on my face couldn't be missed.

After all that, cosmetics were pretty much anticlimactic, and the makeup artist couldn't do much with my eyes anyway, so soon after the laser thing. Lisa started looking at her watch a lot, and there wasn't much time to shop for clothes, but we hit one boutique, where I tried on some tight jeans and a rhinestone-encrusted midriff-baring tee, just this side of trashy.

"Fabulous," Lisa proclaimed when I emerged from the dressing room. But this time, when I caught a glimpse of myself in a mirror, I had some doubts. It seemed to me that even the most open-minded politician in the world wouldn't want her daughter looking like she was up for sale.

"I don't know, Lisa. I think it's a little too much. And what I really need is something to wear for the dinner tonight with my mother."

"Didn't you bring anything with you from school?"

"Just a boring old shirtdress. I don't think it's nice enough for a restaurant. Are we going out?"

"Sounds perfect," Lisa said hurriedly, not answering my question. She looked at her watch again. "Ohmigod, look at the time. We've got to go." She didn't even give me time to change back into what I'd been wearing; she just told the salesgirl to cut off the tags.

On the way back, Lisa seemed preoccupied, which was okay by me, since I didn't particularly want a conversation. I was too busy trying to come up with a believable fantasy of Margaret Hunsucker's reaction to my new look. It was impossible. How could I anticipate the reaction of someone I apparently didn't know at all? I couldn't make any sense out of anything. But I knew this: For the first time since maybe forever, I was actually excited about seeing her. Whoever this woman was, whatever she really stood for, she had to be pretty unusual to let me be me like this. I felt like I was about to be introduced to my mother for the very first time.

But it seemed I would have to wait a little longer before meeting this extraordinary woman. She wasn't back at the house yet. In fact, no one was around. "It's so hard to get staff to stay on a Saturday evening," Lisa murmured, even though I hadn't asked for an explanation. But I did notice the absence of all those security guards I'd seen earlier—Secret Service, men in black, whatever they were—and I mentioned this to Lisa.

"Oh, they're around," she assured me. "This is a pretty big estate, you know. Don't worry, they're watching us even when we can't see them."

"I'm not worried," I told her. "I was just curious."

"Are you tired?" Lisa asked. "Want to lie down for a while?"

"Not really," I replied. "What's the plan for tonight, anyway?"

"Oh, the usual," she said vaguely.

"The usual *what*?" I asked. "I've never had a birthday with my mother."

26

"Oh, of course, how stupid of me," Lisa said quickly. "Well, she thought you'd like something low-key. A nice dinner together here at home, a cake, a few friends—"

"Whose friends?" I didn't have any friends around here, and I didn't know any of hers.

"Just, you know, *friends*." She almost sounded impatient with my questions, but she recovered quickly. "Sorry, I guess *I'm* a little tired. How about some tea?"

She fixed it in the kitchen, and then called me in. We sat at a little table, and she kept glancing at the door. "Are you worried?" I asked her.

"About what?"

"Well, maybe my mother isn't going to be thrilled with my makeover."

"She'll love it," Lisa stated. Then she managed a smile. "You do look fantastic, you know."

"Thanks," I said, and as I spoke a yawn escaped.

"See, you *are* tired," Lisa said. "You know where your room is, don't you? Why don't you go lie down for a while? If you fall asleep, I'll wake you in plenty of time to get ready for tonight."

I shrugged. "Okay." I wasn't really tired, but I didn't like the tea, and Lisa was clearly not in such a great mood anymore. I had a pretty good feeling she was afraid that we'd overdone my new look, and that she just might be in for some grief from her boss.

I went to the bedroom Lisa had called "my" room, though I didn't think of it that way. I'd only slept in it a couple of times. But all my stuff from all the rooms I'd lived in since I was little had been dragged here, so I spent a few minutes moving around and reacquainting myself with—well, myself, I guess.

There were some old favorite books on the bookshelf,

and a stack of board games—Monopoly, Clue, stuff like that. I remembered those well, since I rarely had anyone to play them with me and usually pretended I was two people so I could have a game.

There were dolls, lots of them, sitting on the little plush velvet settee against the wall, decorating the mantel over the fireplace. There were dolls on the bed, dolls on top of the bookcase, and one enormous life-sized doll stuck in a corner of the room. As I recalled, the life-sized one had an extensive wardrobe of clothes, grander and fancier than most life-sized people, with matching bags and shoes. She'd been the gift of some foreign ambassador, I think.

They were all gifts, these dolls, these talking dolls, walking dolls, fashion dolls, dolls dressed in the native costumes of other countries. Gifts from senators, members of the House of Representatives, governors, mayors. I was pretty sure that the baby doll wrapped in the pink blanket came from a president.

But the vast majority had come in birthday and Christmas wrapping paper, and had been accompanied by a card that read "Merry Christmas, Jessica," or "Happy birthday to my darling daughter," followed by "Love, Mother." I probably still had the cards somewhere, too, and what someone might find interesting is that the handwritings were all different. I doubt that she ever signed one herself.

They didn't look particularly well loved, these dolls—in fact, most of them looked practically brand-new. That was because I didn't like dolls, I'd never liked dolls, I was totally uninterested in them. I could forgive the dignitaries and politicians for giving me dolls—after all, they assumed all little girls would like a doll. But my mother should have known I wasn't crazy about them.

On the other hand, she didn't know anything about me. So why should she know what I played with?

Despite the dolls, it was a nice big room on the second floor, with a huge double bed, and a little seating area with a small sofa and a rocking chair. There was an attached private bathroom, too. I went in there to have another look in a mirror.

An odd scratchy noise made me twitch for a minute, but then I could see where it was coming from. Just outside the bathroom window was a large tree, and a wind was making its branches hit the glass. The sun was going down, and the image of the waving branches was just a little creepy.

I took off my cardboard glasses—the doctor had said I only had to leave them on till six—and my eyes looked fine. I was tempted to take the bandage off my arm, too, but the tattoo guy had said to leave it there for at least five hours. The piercings were okay—nothing was red or puffy. Having never been a vain type, since I'd never had looks that might make me conceited, it felt totally weird and amazing to be really admiring myself in the mirror. It was like a fantasy come true—I looked cool. I debated getting out the new makeup and doing some kohl-rimmed eyes, but then I yawned again and realized I was actually a little sleepy.

Looking back now, I'm guessing there had probably been something in that tea. But at that moment, I just felt pleasantly drowsy, and it wasn't until I lay on my bed that I realized I was completely exhausted. My head hit the pillow and I was out.

When I opened my eyes again, the room was dark. Lisa must have come in and closed the curtains, I thought, but as I struggled to a semi-upright position, I could see that the curtains were still open—it was just completely dark outside.

What time was it? I wondered. My mind felt mushy. There was nothing wrong with my eyesight, though. I could make out the bedside clock—both hands were on the twelve.

Which even my foggy brain acknowledged couldn't possibly be right. I saw my backpack, still lying on the little sofa where I'd dropped it when I came in the room. And next to the sofa, the rocking chair.

Rocking. With someone sitting in it.

"Lisa? . . . Mother?" But, with my radically improved vision, I knew it was neither of them. Even though a shadow covered the figure in the rocking chair, I could see that it was a man. And as he rose from the chair, I could see that he was older than me but not *old,* maybe twenty. And dark-haired. A Secret Service man?

But I was pretty sure that Secret Service men didn't wear long red cloaks. I sat up.

It's bizarre how normal your voice can sound when you're scared out of your wits.

"Who are you? What are you doing here?"

"I'll explain later," he said. "It's time to go."

Was it possible that he was a chauffeur? I didn't think so.

"Go where?"

"I can't get into all that now. Just get up and come with me." He sounded impatient.

I took a deep breath and considered screaming. Hadn't Lisa told me those Secret Service guys were all over the place? But would they get to me before this character could take out whatever weapon he carried and use it on me?

"Tell me now," I said, "who you are and where you want to take me."

"It doesn't matter," he said, and he almost sounded like he was getting annoyed with me. "We don't have time for all these questions now; just get up and take my hand."

I swung my legs over the side of the bed, but I didn't stand. "I don't know who you are. Why would I go anywhere with you?"

He let out an irritated sigh. "Because you don't have a choice. You belong to me. Now, come *on*."

Great. A psycho kidnapper. My heart was now beating so hard and fast it actually hurt. I tried to think. The guy wasn't larger than life, but he was bigger than me. Even if he didn't have a weapon, he could hurt me, he could take me by force. But what he'd just said—"You belong to me"—told me he couldn't be sane, he wasn't doing this just for the ransom money. I had to stay calm, get him to talk, stall for time until the guards or Lisa or *somebody* came. I was in the house of a candidate for president of the United States, for crying out loud. There had to be someone around.

"So . . . you own me," I said. "How—how did that happen?"

"Your mother. She sold you." He patted his long red cape. "I've got the receipt here somewhere."

"That's okay, I don't need to see it," I said quickly. "So . . . you've come to collect me."

"Exactly, and it's a long trip, so I'd appreciate it if you could get moving."

Play along, just play along, my brain instructed. "Okay. . . . Do you mind if I use the bathroom first?"

"Go ahead, just be quick about it."

I edged by him and got a glimpse of his face. Even in my panic, I didn't think he looked particularly frightening. Or even nuts.

I took my backpack from the sofa. "I, uh, need some, you know, female stuff," I offered as explanation.

He made an odd little sound and averted his eyes, as if I'd embarrassed him. I moved into the bathroom, where I coughed loudly so he wouldn't hear the click as I locked the door. Slipping the backpack straps over my shoulders, I put down the lid of the toilet and climbed up on it. Standing there,

I was able to reach the window, and to my relief, it opened easily and noiselessly. I was now very pleased to have that bare, creepy tree within grabbing distance. I got hold of a sturdy-looking limb, planted a foot on the angle where it met the trunk, and hauled myself out the window.

I felt my way down to the limb below it, but then I couldn't feel another heavy branch. I stretched my leg as far as it could go while still keeping one leg on the limb, but there was nothing to step onto. I had no idea how far down I'd come, or what distance I was from the ground, and I could only hope it wasn't a bone-breaking one. I dangled my legs for a few seconds, and then I dropped.

chapter
Three

IT WASN'T BAD. I hit the ground on my knees, but it didn't feel like I'd done any damage. I certainly wasn't going to take the time to look, and besides, there wasn't any light. I thought about yelling, to draw the attention of one of those invisible Secret Service guys who were supposed to be lurking all over the place. But I didn't dare—the maniac in my bedroom was more than likely lurking even closer.

It was pitch-black outside, but way off in the distance I made out some streetlights, and I took off in that direction. I recalled my arrival that morning—we'd taken an exit off the highway, then traveled a short distance before turning into the long driveway that led to the house. The lights I could see probably came from the highway, and it had to be pretty far away, but I felt reasonably sure one of the security guys would cross my path before I got there.

I encountered no one at all. There wasn't even anyone in the guardhouse. I paused every now and then, to catch my breath and to listen for a potential savior—or for the psycho, who might already be chasing me. But I heard nothing, not until I was close enough to the highway to hear an occasional car. When I finally arrived, I waved frantically at a car, but it whizzed by without even slowing down.

At least I was out in public now, and it felt safe to stop for a minute. I fumbled in my backpack and pulled out my cell phone. No network. Another car was coming, and once again I tried to flag it down, but to no avail. On the other side of the highway, I saw a turnoff with a sign that read MOTEL. I dashed across and headed in that direction.

It was a pretty seedy-looking place, a shabby row of eight connected units covered in peeling pink paint, but I figured there had to be someone on duty, and a telephone. There was a light on in the first cottage, and as I approached it, I made out the word "Reception" over the door.

A young but grizzled guy was leaning back in a chair, his feet up on the desk. He glanced in my direction as I entered, staring at my bare stomach, but he said nothing, just blinked in acknowledgment of my presence. Then he took a long drag off a stinky-smelling hand-rolled cigarette that just had to contain something other than tobacco, which could have accounted for his apparent inability to focus.

"Hello. Can I use your phone, please?"

He muttered something unintelligible, but it was accompanied by a shake of his head, which made the negative meaning clear.

"Then could you call the police?" I asked. "I'm in trouble—someone's after me!"

I wasn't sure if that had sunk in. His eyes had moved to the corner behind me. I whirled around, half expecting to see the crazy would-be kidnapper approaching the cottage, but realized that the guy was looking at a TV. The sound had been turned down, but there was an image on the screen. An image I recognized immediately.

Senator Margaret Hunsucker stood in front of the house I'd just escaped from. A replay of her presidential-candidacy announcement? But, no, across the bottom of the screen ran the words "BREAKING NEWS . . . BREAKING NEWS . . . BREAK-ING NEWS."

"Could you turn up the sound, please?" I asked.

"Huh?"

The remote was on the desk, so I picked it up and hit the "volume" button. My mother's voice filled the room.

"Only another mother can know how I'm feeling right now." She sounded as if she was choking on the words. "All I can do is appeal to the kidnappers. Please, please, let my daughter go." She then collapsed into the arms of some man standing behind her who yelled, "No more questions, please!"

Now the camera was on another man, who stood off to the side of the house. "That was Senator Margaret Hunsucker, pleading for the release of her daughter, Jessica, who was kidnapped from her home less than an hour ago. According to a spokesperson for the senator, international terrorists are suspected of playing a part in this act."

And there was Lisa, looking much as she had when I'd left her, only not smiling. "Everyone knows that Senator Hunsucker takes a hard line on terrorism. We believe that a certain group has targeted the senator, and that they will make demands that would benefit their evil agenda before they will free her daughter. If they are watching this broadcast, let them know this now. The United States of America does not deal, negotiate, or bargain with terrorists. As a citizen, a patriot, and one who represents this great nation of ours, the senator will only accept the unconditional release of Jessica Hunsucker."

"Ohmigod." I whirled around and faced the stoner. "They're talking about me!"

"Huh?"

"Me! I'm Jessica Hunsucker. Someone just tried to kidnap me, but I got away!"

I might as well have told him I was an alien visitor from Mars. He stared at me blankly.

"I have to call home, right now!" I reached for the phone, but apparently the receptionist was more protective of that instrument than he'd been with the remote control. He snatched up the phone before I could even get close, and nodded toward a sign that read TV AND PHONE IN EVERY ROOM.

"You want a phone, get a room," he said.

I'd rarely used the credit card I'd been given by someone on my mother's staff when I'd first gone away to school at age twelve, and I worried it might have expired. Fortunately, the guy barely glanced at it, but he took it from me. "I have to keep it till you check out," he said before tossing me a key. "Number three."

The door to unit number three opened easily when I turned the key, but that was the only thing in the musty-smelling room that seemed to work. I hit the switch by the door, but only one feeble, blinking light came on. Spotting the remote control, I aimed it at the TV to see if there was any more news about my kidnapping, but nothing happened. I picked up the phone, and it was dead. I wasted a couple of seconds punching the 0, and then went back outside.

By now, I was feeling so frustrated that I wasn't even frightened anymore. All I could think about was my poor mother, that nice Lisa, all those people thinking that I'd been kidnapped and that I was in mortal danger, and here I was, perfectly safe and sound, and I couldn't even let them know! I stormed back into the reception unit.

The TV was still on, with sound, and the freak at the desk was staring at it. "The phone in the room isn't working," I declared.

His eyes slowly drifted toward me. "I'll tell the manager when he comes in tomorrow."

"Whatever, but I need a phone *now*!" This time I didn't wait for a response. I reached out and put my hand on the phone. For a guy who was stoned out of his mind, he moved fast, slamming his own hand on top of mine.

"We interrupt this program for a special bulletin."

He loosened his grip, and I could have picked up the phone, but the image on the screen grabbed my attention. We were back in front of the Hunsucker house, and the reporter was speaking again.

"This is Roger Searle at the home of senator and presidential candidate Margaret Hunsucker," the man said. "Apparently, there has been a tragic development in the suspected kidnapping of the senator's daughter. We have just been informed that a body identified as Jessica Hunsucker has been discovered in the wooded area right in front of the house. The area had been thoroughly searched in the moments immediately following Jessica's disappearance, so it would seem that somehow the perpetrators of this horrific act managed to return to the scene undetected. How they were able to accomplish this, with the house surrounded by investigators and Secret Service, is unknown. But Senator Hunsucker has positively identified the body as her missing daughter, and she is now in seclusion."

And then Lisa was on the screen. "This is the consequence of the senator's refusal to deal with terrorists. This barbaric act, the cold-blooded murder of Jessica Hunsucker. . . ."

Somehow, in my state of total confusion, I noticed that my credit card was still on the desk. I jabbed my finger at it. "Can't you read? What's the name on this credit card?"

His eyes had actually begun to clear, and he made out the

words: "Jessica Hunsucker." He blinked. "You're supposed to be dead."

"Yeah, well, obviously, I'm *not*. Could you *please* call the police?"

He picked up the phone and dialed.

Lisa was still on TV. "Jessica has become a martyr in the war against terrorism. And even in her grief, the senator has asked me to convey to all those who have suffered, who have faced the threat of terrorism, who have lost loved ones in this ongoing battle, her renewed commitment to uncover and destroy the forces that threaten us daily, and that today took the life of an innocent sixteen-year-old girl." Now the screen was covered with a film of—me. It must have been taken that morning, when I arrived. I was getting out of the car in my oversized and wrinkled T-shirt, my long dark hair in a tangled mess, my glasses slipping down the bridge of my nose. . . .

And I realized that now the eyes of the receptionist had widened and brightened and were darting between the image on the screen and me in the flesh. Me. With platinum-blond spiky hair and a midriff-baring top. He looked again at the credit card. I snatched it off the desk and jammed it into the pocket of my jeans, but it was too late. He'd seen enough, and I knew what he was thinking.

"That's me," I insisted, pointing to the screen. "I just had a haircut."

He spoke into the phone. "Police? Is this the police?"

"Let me talk to them," I demanded, reaching for the phone, but he jumped out of his seat and stepped back.

"I got one of those terrorists here! Right here in front of me!"

"Are you crazy?" I screamed, but he kept yelling into the phone.

"One of those terrorists that just killed the girl! The senator's kid!"

I turned and ran out. All I could think of now was to get myself back home, where at least Lisa could recognize and identify me. It took me a while to get across the highway and onto the driveway that led to the house. I didn't get very far.

A police car was right behind me, and another one came down the driveway from the house. Sirens wailed and lights flashed, and then, from out of nowhere, a dozen Secret Service types appeared on either side of me with their guns drawn.

"On the ground!" someone yelled.

I froze.

"On the ground or we'll shoot!"

I knew they really would, too. But I couldn't move; I couldn't speak. Then I heard another voice, softer and closer, just behind me.

"Can we please go *now*?"

It was the voice from my bedroom. I still couldn't move, but I felt his hand take mine.

"Okay?" he asked.

"Okay," I whispered.

The sirens faded, the lights dimmed, the police all around me started to become blurry . . . or maybe it was me, just floating away.

Chapter
Four

I FIGURED I was still suffering from the effects of whatever Lisa put in the tea. In any case, time must have passed by the time I realized I was in the passenger seat of a car.

I recognized my kidnapper at the wheel. Quickly, before he could see that I was awake, I shut my eyes, performed what I hoped looked like a sleep movement in order to face in the opposite direction, and opened my eyes again.

Looking out the window, I thought I recognized the passing scene, though I couldn't put a name to it. Leafy Meadows, Crystal Pines, something like that. Or maybe I'd never even been on this particular street before, but it was definitely familiar. We were in a suburb, with evenly spaced small houses painted in grayish pastels. They weren't identical—some were a little bigger, others were split-level—but they all had a tired, unloved look. There were crooked venetian blinds at the windows, no flower boxes or hanging baskets by the front doors, and the paint on the shutters was peeling.

The community wasn't into landscaping or gardening, either. The plots in front of the houses were shabby—sparse, spotty patches of lawn, a sickly-looking tree or two—and the only decorations on the lawns were the occasional gnomes, who looked just a little grimmer than the usual ones.

There were no sidewalks. No signs of life, either—but from the look of the sky, it must have been shortly after dawn, and it was a Sunday, I remembered. In any case, there was no one I could wave to or signal that I needed help. But we'd have to come to a stop sign or a red light eventually, and that was when I could try for an escape. I wasn't tied up, I wasn't even wearing a seat belt, so I thought I could get out of the car pretty quickly. Of course, there was the possibility that the door was childproof, locked by a mechanism that only the driver could control. Or my captor might have a gun, and I wouldn't even make it to one of those front doors we were passing.

On the other hand, if he killed me, he wouldn't have any bargaining power for a ransom . . . and for the first time, I wondered why in the world I'd chosen abduction over being arrested. Those cops might have looked scary, but eventually they would have learned the truth about me. So why did I take this crazy guy's hand? It was insane, it made absolutely no sense at all . . . yet somehow it had seemed right. But I couldn't waste time pondering my stupid act. I needed to think about what I could do now.

I did another moving-in-my-sleep body shift in order to get a peek at him. Unfortunately, just as I opened my eyes, he took his eyes momentarily off the road to look directly at me.

"Hi."

"Hello," I replied. There was a moment of silence. "Um . . . where are we?"

He glanced out at the boring landscape. "Hell."

I could see what he meant. If I lived in a neighborhood like this, that was what I'd call it. I remembered some old techno song about "suburban hell." Pet Shop Boys, maybe. I decided to risk asking another question. "So . . . what's the plan?"

"Huh?"

"What's going to happen now?"

He shrugged. "I just thought we'd see how it goes."

I wanted to know how much money he was going to demand for me, but I was afraid that might be too personal. Still, I wanted to keep a conversation going, so I asked something else that was bothering me. "Whose body was tossed on my mother's lawn?"

"No idea," he said. "She could have stolen a body from a morgue for all I know. That was your mother's plan, not mine."

Jeez, he really was nuts. I tried to look him over without staring. He didn't *look* crazy. In the darkness of my bedroom, in the red cloak, he'd been a little scary. Now I could see that he was actually pretty ordinary-looking—short, curly brown hair, roundish face, wire-rimmed glasses. Narrow shoulders, sort of scrawny. He wore a light-blue shirt and jeans. I turned my head and saw the long red cape crumpled on the back seat of the car.

If I'd seen him on a street, I'd have thought he was a college student, intelligent, not very athletic. Maybe a techie. Kind of cute, though, in a nerdy way.

He looked nervous, or uncertain, so I knew I had to be careful. I'd read a self-defense article in a teen magazine once. It said that if the person threatening you seemed nervous, he could be a first-time criminal, not a pro. It advised the victim to keep him talking, so maybe he'd relax and let down his guard. But not to say anything upsetting, which might make him react violently. So what was I supposed to talk to him about? Ask him about his favorite band, football, where he went to school?

I tried to sound offhand and conversational. "So—you said the kidnapping was my mother's plan. That's interesting. Why would she do that?"

"You got me. Probably for some political reason, I guess. Maybe she thinks she'll get more votes if people feel sorry for her. Like I said, I had nothing to do with it."

I knew I was supposed to stay calm, but his "I'm so innocent" pose was annoying me. "What do you mean, you had nothing to do with it? You're the one who kidnapped me!"

He glanced at me, and I could have sworn he actually looked offended. "I did *not*! You *belong* to me."

"Oh, right, you said that before, in my room." I jumped back to casual, nonthreatening mode. "Sorry. Okay, I belong to you, you own me, but I'm curious . . . how did that come about?"

"I thought I already told you that, too. Your mother, she sold you to me. Well, not exactly to *me*, but it's the same thing."

"Who exactly did she sell me to?"

"The devil."

"The devil, right. And, um, when did this sale take place?"

"Oh, way before you were born. She made a pact with the devil. He could have her firstborn daughter, and in return he'd give her power."

"Power," I repeated. "What kind of power?"

"Political power, of course. And you can't say the devil hasn't kept his part of the deal. I mean, your mother was a total nobody. First he arranges for her to meet your father, the lieutenant governor. Then he makes the old guy die so she can take his place. And how do you think she won all those elections? She didn't do a damned thing. And now she's going to be president of the United States."

"You think she's going to win?"

"Of course she'll win! You can say what you want about Satan—he follows through on his promises."

I kept talking like all this made perfectly good sense. "But if she sold me way back then, why didn't Satan take me when I was born?"

He shook his head. "We don't take babies. Too messy. No little children, actually. We take girls when they're sixteen, boys at eighteen."

"Because girls mature faster?"

"Exactly."

"So . . . my mother sold me to the devil in exchange for political power. And you are . . . ?"

"Brad. Want some music?" He turned on the radio, and the car was filled with Céline Dion singing the theme to *Titanic*. I was having a bad enough day already; I didn't need this.

"Uh, no thanks."

Obligingly, he turned it off.

"Brad," I repeated. "And how did you end up with me, Brad? I mean, why didn't the devil come for me himself?"

He shot me an aggrieved look. "What's the matter, you think I'm not good enough for you?"

"Oh, no, nothing like that! I was just, you know, curious."

He didn't seem really appeased, but he answered me. "Do you have any idea how many people sell their kids to the devil?"

"So they can be presidents of the United States?"

"*No.* Lots of reasons. Might be for money, or love, or fame. We get a lot more daughters than sons, though. I heard about one girl who promised Satan her first daughter if she could be Miss America. Or Miss Universe, one of those things. Believe me, the devil doesn't need any more chicks. So he hands them off to guys like me."

"Then you're, like, one of the devil's minions?"

"I'm a demon."

"Oh, okay." I looked the other way, out the window. More dull houses and sparse lawns. "And this is Hell."

"Yeah."

"It's not the way I pictured it. Where's the fire and brimstone?"

"This is one of the better neighborhoods. For people who committed the smaller deadly sins. Or the ones like you, who got sold."

"So I'm not going to run into someone like—I don't know—Hitler?"

"Nah."

"But this is still Hell."

"Yeah. And this is home." He pulled off the road into a driveway that led to a small white house, no better or worse than the others we'd passed. We both got out of the car, and Brad strode on ahead. He opened the front door, then stepped aside and let me enter first.

The room was dark. Brad hit a switch, and a harsh fluorescent light illuminated it. I looked around.

I was standing on wall-to-wall shag carpeting, in a shade somewhere between beige and gray. Facing me was a long turquoise sofa—it looked like some kind of leatherette or plastic—with a couple of tears in the cushions. On either side of the sofa stood small end tables made of fake-looking blond wood. There was also a worn-out armchair covered in some sort of orange-and-turquoise print fabric. A vase filled with obviously plastic flowers sat on a coffee table.

There were two paintings on the walls. Over the sofa, a group of dogs played cards at a table. On the other wall, two children, a boy and a girl, stared blankly at me through oversized eyes that covered half their faces.

It was the ugliest room I'd ever seen.

"Dining room's over there," Brad said, pointing. "And the kitchen's just beyond." I caught a glimpse of avocado-green appliances.

I wasn't sure at what point my head began to throb, when his words began to sink in and I actually started to hear what he was saying. It didn't hit me like a ton of bricks, it was more like I was slowly absorbing it. It just sort of seeped into my conscious-ness and welled up. But it was right around then that I knew everything he was telling me was true. I froze, and gasped.

Brad didn't notice. "Bedrooms are down that hall," he said, nodding in the opposite direction. "There are two, a master bedroom and a guest room."

"Am I a guest?" I asked in a whisper.

"Well . . . no. You live here now."

In Hell. I was in Hell. And my mother had sent me here. My mother. Margaret Hunsucker, who wanted to be presi-dent so much she was willing to sacrifice her own daughter.

Lisa . . . she had to have been in on it, too. That was the reason for the makeover, so no one would recognize me as the kidnapped daughter of the senator. She'd certainly put on a good act.

Looking back now, I don't know how to describe what I was feeling at that moment. To be faced with something so totally unbelievable and yet to know that it was real, to con-front horror in such an ordinary setting—I couldn't breathe, I couldn't think. Terror swept over me like a tidal wave, and I was drowning.

I didn't know what was more terrible, the fact that I was in Hell or the fact that my mother had put me there. My mother, my mother . . . maybe she'd never been very mater-nal, but she *was* my mother. And mothers loved their daugh-ters. They didn't sell their daughters to the devil.

"*She* should go to Hell," I cried out passionately, "not me. She belongs here."

He actually tried to comfort me. "You never know, she might end up down here. But I don't make those kinds of decisions."

His words were floating over my head, he could have been speaking in another language, they didn't make any sense. I began to cry.

Brad watched me nervously. "It's not that bad, really!" he said. "Look!" He was pointing to a large television in the corner of the room. "I've got cable! And . . . and you'll never get any older, and you can eat all you want and not gain weight. The food's not too great, but . . ."

The sobs were coming out louder now, fueled by utter bewilderment and fear, and I could feel the panic building. Brad looked really upset. He put an arm awkwardly around my shoulders, but I shrank from the demon's touch. He stood there for a moment, and then, gently, he motioned me down the hall. "Why don't you go in there and . . . lie down or something. It's the *guest* room," he added hastily.

On the edge of hysteria and blinded by tears, I stumbled into the room and collapsed on the bed.

chapter
Five

I LAY THERE for some time, but I didn't sleep.

Sleep usually came easily to me. My head would hit the pillow and—boom—I was out. And if I was really tired, I could fall asleep just about anywhere, even sitting on a hard chair in a classroom under bright lights while a teacher was giving a lecture.

And sleep had always been an easy refuge for me, too. When I was depressed, or anxious, I could always escape my problems by going to sleep. It was only a temporary solution, but it was better than nothing.

But here I lay in the demon's guest room, completely exhausted, utterly despondent, and more frightened than I'd ever been in my life, but I couldn't sleep. The awfulness of my life was now beyond anything I could cope with in any way whatsoever. There was no getting away from it, physically or mentally. I was completely lost, overwhelmed by the bizarre enormity of the situation.

I was without hope. Even suicide wasn't an escape option. Because I was in Hell—which, I assumed, meant that I was already dead.

Brad stood in the doorway. "Do you want something to eat? Or drink?"

"No, thank you," I replied automatically.

"Okay, well . . . I have to go out for a little while. Make yourself at home. There are some books, and I, um, programmed the TV for you in case you feel like watching."

I probably mumbled another thank you, but he didn't hear me. I turned and saw that he was still standing there.

"You can't run away, you know." His tone was almost apologetic. "There's nothing to run to."

"I know." My words came out in a whisper, but he heard me this time.

"Well . . . see ya soon."

A moment later, I heard the front door open and close. I remained still. When I was absolutely, positively sure that sleep wouldn't take me away, I got up.

Back in the living room, I noticed for the first time the small bookcase in a corner. I crouched down to examine the titles.

Functions of Photosynthesis.

Renal Failure in Sedentary Populations.

Dictionary of Legal Terminology.

Cholesterol-Free Cooking.

It was like being in a secondhand bookstore, where you waded through dull, ancient books and hoped to be rewarded eventually for your efforts with something you'd always meant to read. But there were no rewards on these two shelves. . . . No, wait! What was this? The words on the spine were faded, but I could make out the name of the author: Agatha Christie. I knew who she was—I'd even read one of her classic mysteries—and I snatched this one off the shelf.

The back cover of the book hung limply, and I could guess why, even before my examination of the binding confirmed my suspicion. An entire section of pages had been torn out. The last section, of course.

A mystery with no resolution. I could read it, get into it,

and never know whodunit. Well, what did I expect? This was Hell.

I wandered into the kitchen, where I saw a bowl of apples on the little breakfast table. I didn't have to touch them to know they were wax. Were there real apples in Hell? I wondered. I recalled what the demon had said, that the food wasn't great. If there *were* apples, I could forget about Granny Smiths. They'd be the mealy kind, with no crisp bite to them. The kind that tasted like baby-food applesauce.

It didn't matter—I wasn't hungry, and I couldn't believe I was even having these stupid thoughts. I just needed something to distract me.

I went back to the living room. I wasn't sure what the demon had meant about having programmed the TV for me, but I took the remote from the coffee table and clicked it on. I blinked when I recognized the image on the screen. It was the soccer field at Woodbridge, my school. There was no one on it, and at first I thought it was a still photo, but then a breeze caused the school banner to flap a little.

When nothing else happened, I hit one of the arrow buttons. Now I saw the Woodbridge auditorium, also vacant. I clicked again, and this time I actually saw a couple of girls by the back door of my dorm. They were sharing a cigarette and furtively looking over their shoulders as they puffed. I didn't know either of them, so it wasn't very interesting. What *was* interesting was that apparently there were surveillance cameras all over the campus. For security purposes, I imagined. Too bad there hadn't been cameras like that back in my bedroom at home.

I hit the button. Now, *this* was interesting—I was actually in someone's room at the residence hall. Was there a camera in everyone's room? I winced as I recalled some of my own activities in my room that I wouldn't have wanted anyone observing.

I fiddled with buttons on the remote, and realized I could get a closer view of the girl sitting at the desk. I recognized her—Emily Something, she'd sat across the aisle from me in calculus. She was turning the pages of a book that looked like a travel guide.

She looked up as another girl came into the room. "I think we're going to have to choose between Venice and Florence," she said. "There's not enough time to do both while we're in Italy."

"Couldn't we do both if we skipped Rome?" the other girl asked.

"We can't skip *Rome!*" Emily exclaimed.

Clearly, they were planning a trip together. Too bad I couldn't watch *that*—I would have liked to see Rome. And Florence, and Venice, and all the places that I always thought I'd visit someday. And now I never would. I'd never see Rome, Paris, London. . . . I'd never go on safari in East Africa or wander around Egyptian pyramids. I thought of experiences I'd had that I would have liked to have again. There would never be another swim in the Atlantic Ocean, no more rides on a Ferris wheel. I wouldn't even drink another iced mocha latte at Starbucks.

The panic was rising inside me again, so I began hitting buttons at random, just to keep myself occupied. I was taken aback when I found myself watching a scene in an unfamiliar kitchen, where a woman I'd never seen before was standing at a stove and stirring something in a pot. A moment later, a man I *did* recognize came in—Mr. Kessler, the American-history teacher at Woodbridge. He was carrying what looked like a grocery bag.

"They only had frozen scallops at the market, no fresh ones, so I got shrimp instead," he said.

"That's fine," the woman, who I presumed was *Mrs.* Kessler, replied. "I hope you remembered the garlic."

"Yes, and the fennel, too."

I wondered what they were making. And then it hit me, what kind of TV they had here in Hell: reality programming. The dumbest kind of TV—no stories, no writers, no actors, just regular people doing whatever they did. And this wasn't even the mildly interesting kind of reality show, with a competition, like *American Idol* or *Project Runway*. This was *real* reality.

I began pressing the channel button again, and my insight was confirmed. I could watch life on earth. So far, I hadn't seen anything worth watching, but I kept surfing, and finally I saw something that made me stop.

It was a room in the house I'd left not too long ago. Senator Margaret Hunsucker sat in a chair, her eyes closed, as some woman swept a large makeup brush over her face.

"I can't tell you how very sorry I am for your loss, Senator," she said.

My mother opened her eyes. I leaned forward and scrutinized them for any trace of a tear. "Thank you."

Lisa entered, and spoke sharply to the makeup girl. "Please don't talk to the senator."

"It's all right, Lisa," my mother said. She spoke kindly to the makeup artist. "But perhaps it's better if we don't discuss Jessica. I'll start crying, and then you'll have to do my eyes all over again."

It was amazing—she really looked sad. Was she that good an actress? For one brief, fleeting second, I thought maybe, just maybe, I'd had it right the first time. Brad wasn't a demon, he was an ordinary kidnapper. The body tossed on the lawn was someone who just looked like me. And I wasn't in Hell, not literally, just some ugly, dreary, but run-of-the-mill suburb.

Wishful thinking. The makeup girl left, and Lisa handed my mother a paper. "Just a few changes."

My mother looked it over. "Yes, this is good. Is everything set up?" She spoke briskly, and then went to a mirror on the wall. "I've been wondering if I should get my hair lightened before the televised debates. What do you think?"

Lisa joined her. "Nothing too dramatic. Maybe just some subtle streaks around your face. It would soften you."

"Yes, that's what I thought. Okay, I'm ready."

Any tiny remnant of hope evaporated. I didn't know much about loss or grief, but I suspected that a woman whose daughter had just died wouldn't be preoccupied with her hair.

I had no idea how this system worked, if some sort of magical invisible camera was following them, but I was able to watch the two of them go outside. In front of the house, reporters and cameras rushed forward. Lisa spoke into a microphone.

"The senator will make one brief statement. She will not take any questions at this time, and we ask that you respect the fact that she is in mourning." She stepped aside and ceded the microphone to her boss.

"I want to inform you all that, yes, my campaign will continue," Margaret Hunsucker said, in a voice that held only the slightest hint of a tremor. "Despite this unspeakable tragedy, I believe I must go on. I owe this to the American people, and to my daughter. This is what she would have wanted. I dedicate my campaign to Jessica, who believed in our cause."

I gasped. How could she say that? She didn't know my views—we'd never discussed anything about her campaign. And then I almost laughed at my outrage. A woman who could send her daughter to Hell wouldn't have any problem making up her daughter's politics.

But I couldn't watch any more of this. I hit the channel button until I returned to Woodbridge. I was back in the auditorium, but now people, students and teachers, occupied the seats. I thought there must have been some sort of required convocation. Ms. Perkins, the headmistress, was at the podium.

"We are gathered here today to honor and celebrate the memory of Jessica Hunsucker. Jessica was here with us at Woodbridge for only a short time, but she left an impact."

That took me aback. I'd always felt pretty much invisible at school. But maybe this was just what people always said at occasions like this.

The door to the house opened, and Brad entered. I turned, and he gave me a tentative smile.

"Anything good on?" he asked, nodding in the direction of the television.

"A memorial for me," I said. "At my school."

He came around to the sofa, and sat down at the other end. "They must miss you."

I shook my head. "They didn't even know me."

Kip Simmonds was at the podium now. "I was the last person to see Jessica before she left campus yesterday. I'll never forget her. She had a wonderful sense of humor."

I rolled my eyes. Personally, I agreed—I did have a sense of humor—but I couldn't remember ever having cracked a joke in *her* presence. And she wasn't the last person to see me on campus. That cute guy, Sanders—did he know I was gone? Did he care?

Brad coughed. "Um, I'm sorry I had to leave you alone here. I guess this has to be pretty traumatic for you. But I had some work I couldn't put off."

Whatever it was, it couldn't have been much fun. He still wore that hangdog, sheepish expression.

I hit the "mute" button and turned to him. "What do demons do, anyway?"

He perked up, as if he was flattered by my interest. "That depends. I'm currently assigned to temptation. Enticements to sin."

I nodded. "You try to get people to do bad things."

"I just put out the bait. I'm in finance at the moment, so mostly I provide opportunities to steal, or embezzle, that sort of thing."

"And that's enough to send a person to Hell?" I asked.

"Well, it's a cumulative thing, you know. Usually, it takes more than one sin. I'm not very high up in the business. I just enable the first temptation."

"And you collect people who were sold to the devil."

"Actually, you were my first. I was next in line for a partner, so . . ." His voice trailed off. "It's supposed to be an incentive for working harder."

"So you're not a big shot in Hell," I commented.

"I haven't been here all that long," he replied.

"Where were you before?"

"Cincinnati. At a university."

"How did you end up here?"

Now he looked distinctly uncomfortable. "Um, I really don't want to talk about it. Not now, okay?"

"But you did something bad, right?"

"Yeah." He looked away.

I looked away, too. "I didn't do anything."

"I know," he said. "It kind of sucks, huh?"

"Definitely." After a few seconds, I asked, "Will I always feel this bad?"

"You get used to it."

My eyes were burning again. I picked up the remote control. "Let's see what else is on."

He brightened. "Hey, you know what you can do? You can watch famous people live. Movie stars, celebrities. Royalty. Name a celebrity."

I named the first one who came to mind. "Madonna."

"Watch." He hit some numbers and pressed "enter." The screen displayed an image of a bed, with someone in it. Sheets obscured the face of the person.

"That's Madonna. Sleeping."

We watched for a minute, but she didn't even move in her sleep.

"Think of someone else," Brad said.

I named the lead singer of a band I liked. The demon entered some numbers. And there he was, the great-looking, long-haired singer, pulling down his pants to sit on a toilet.

"I really don't want to see this," I said.

"Can't blame you." He went back to Madonna. She was still sleeping. "Sometimes you have to do a lot of surfing before you hit something good," he explained. "Anyone else?"

"Paris Hilton," I suggested.

"Who?"

Obviously, he'd been dead for a while now. I tried to think of someone else, like Madonna, who'd been famous for a long time. But Brad came up with a suggestion first.

"Want to see what your mother's up to?"

I didn't tell him I'd already had a look at her. I didn't want to admit I was even interested in her. I said nothing, but he took that as an okay.

She was in a meeting now, sitting at the head of a table. Lisa was there, and three men. "You need to get right back on the road," one of the men said to the senator.

"Won't that look kind of cold?" Lisa asked. "People expect her to be depressed."

"It doesn't matter," one of the other men said. "I mean, you're going to win no matter what you do. That's part of the deal, right?"

Margaret Hunsucker spoke. "Yes, of course, but it's not just the winning. We need to start planning for after the election. We've got our goals, we know what we want, but we need to work on the specifics, how exactly we're going to reach these goals."

Lisa looked up at her in pure adoration. "How you're going to change the country."

My mother smiled. "How I'm going to change the world."

AT THAT MOMENT, two men in white aprons pushed food carts into the conference room. Lunch was served, people began talking to each other, and the conversations became muffled and inaudible.

"So she's going to change the world," Brad commented.

I brushed that off. "She's a politician. They all talk like that."

"Yeah, I guess you're right. I never paid much attention to politics."

I had to remind myself that he'd been human once, and I tried to work up some interest in that fact. It might take my mind off myself. "What were you into?"

"Computers, mainly. I guess I was kind of what they call a computer geek. But this was in the eighties," he added hastily. "Before everyone had the Internet and e-mail."

"How *old* are you?"

"I guess I'd say I'm nineteen. Like I told you, you don't get older here. You just stay the same age you were when you . . . when you arrived."

When you died. That was what he really meant, he just didn't want to remind me. Which was kind of sweet.

I could have pursued this line of questioning and found out more about Brad, but I didn't have the energy. "What time is it anyway? Wait . . . do you have time here? I mean, if people don't get older . . ."

"It's not *real* time, like what you're used to," he admitted. "But it's *like* time. They try to make the conditions feel like earth, with day and night, light and dark. So it's a little more comfortable. But only in nice areas like this," he added. "There are parts of Hell that are completely dark all the time."

I supposed that was interesting, but it was the word "they" that stuck in my mind. Did he actually mean "he"? "So—who makes those kinds of decisions? Are you talking about"—I took a deep breath—"Satan?"

Brad winced. "We don't have to get into that now. You need to relax and settle in before you start learning all the bureaucratic crap. Hey, want to eat something?"

Having not eaten since I arrived, I knew I should be hungry, though I wasn't sure what I was feeling yet. I wasn't even sure if physical conditions like hunger existed in Hell. But eating would be something to do.

"Okay."

"I was thinking we could take a ride over to McDonald's."

I could see that he enjoyed the surprise on my face. "You have McDonald's here?"

"You didn't expect that, huh? It's what you'd call ironic. I told you the food wasn't any good, right? Well, that's based on what's considered good food by gourmet types, what do they call 'em now, foodies, you know what I mean? People who are into quality and healthy stuff, people who like to cook and go to fancy restaurants. So, if that kind of person ends up here, and he sees what's available to eat, he knows he's in Hell. But for the rest of us, it's okay! Pretty cool, huh?"

I wasn't a huge fan of fast food, but I could see what he meant. "So there are Big Macs in Hell."

"Oh, we've got 'em all. KFC, Taco Bell . . . I'm just hoping the higher-ups never figure out that some of us are happy about that."

"The higher-ups?"

"Administrative types." He gave me a lopsided grin. "Maybe I should call them the lower-downs."

I couldn't help smiling. It wasn't that funny, but I suppose you couldn't expect a demon to have a very sophisticated sense of humor. "Okay, let's go to McDonald's."

We went back outside and got into the car. Automatically, I reached for the seat belt, but there wasn't one. Which made sense, I guess—you wouldn't need a seat belt to protect you if you were already dead. As Brad pulled out of the driveway, I noticed a woman sitting on the steps of the house next door and smoking a cigarette—something else you wouldn't have to worry about in this place. She looked like she might have been in her thirties. Clearly she hadn't died of old age. She waved as we drove by, and Brad made a gesture of salute toward her.

"Who's that?" I asked.

"Her name's Angie."

"Why is she here?"

"Killed her husband, I think."

"Oh. Wouldn't murder put you in a nastier part of Hell?"

Brad shrugged. "Maybe she had a good excuse."

"Like self-defense? You don't go to Hell for killing someone in self-defense, do you?"

"Depends."

"On what?"

"I don't know." He took his eyes off the road just long enough to give me an apologetic look. "It's not my department. Here we are."

Whoever was in charge of fast food in Hell had done a

pretty good job of replicating the Golden Arches. There were the standard booths and tables, the long counter at the back, and the usual overflowing trash bins. The place seemed a little less noisy than a typical McDonald's, though, and I quickly figured out why.

"There are no kids here."

"No. Like I told you, we don't take children."

"Oh, right." There were teenagers, though, as customers and behind the counter taking orders, and they seemed exactly right for the setting. It occurred to me that all the people I'd ever seen behind the counter in this kind of place looked like they were in Hell.

"Why don't you grab that booth, and I'll get the food," Brad said. "What do you want?"

I automatically gave him my standard McDonald's order. "Um, a small McNuggets and a Diet Coke."

"Fries?"

"No thanks."

"You can't gain any weight here, remember?"

"Okay, fries. And a *real* Coke."

Brad went to the counter; I slid into the booth and checked out the customers around me. Except for the absence of children, the patrons of this McDonald's didn't look particularly unusual. A couple of thirty-something women were engaged in a conversation over coffees, an older man sat alone and stared into space as he twisted the straw in his drink. There were three bored teenagers sitting together but not saying much, sharing a large order of fries and dragging them through a puddle of ketchup on a paper plate.

I've never been a religious person. I could remember being dragged to church once in a while when I was younger, but, knowing what I know now about my mother, I'm sure it was just for publicity. A lot of her followers were probably churchgoers. In any case, I didn't go to Sunday school or get any sort of religious instruction. I suppose I believed in some sort of higher power, though I'd never given Him/Her/It much thought.

But somewhere in the back of my head, I think I always believed there was an afterlife, a Heaven and a Hell. Angels with halos and wings flying around among the clouds up there, nasty little red imps with pitchforks in hand down there. Down *here*. And I'd always assumed that as long as you were basically good, or at least okay, you went to Heaven. You didn't have to be a saint to join the angels, but you'd have to be truly evil to go the other way.

But as I looked around me, all I could think was that everyone looked so ordinary. I couldn't believe that everyone in this restaurant had been either a serial killer or the master-mind behind some ethnic-cleansing program. And surely they couldn't all have been sold, like me.

I brought this up when my demon returned with the food.

"Brad . . . see those teenagers over there?"

"Yeah, what about them?"

"I was just wondering why they're here."

Brad put my tray down in front of me. "Teenagers love fast food."

"No, I mean, why are they in Hell? What could they have done that was so bad?"

Brad unwrapped his Quarter Pounder and took a bite. As he chewed, he gazed speculatively at the group of teens.

He swallowed. "I dunno. Drugs, maybe."

"You can go to Hell just for taking drugs?"

"Maybe they were dealing, too."

"Okay, but what about those women? They look like soccer moms."

"So?"

"So what did they do to get here?"

"How should I know? It's none of my business."

"But aren't you curious?" I pressed.

He put his burger down. "Look, the only reason I know about my neighbor Angie is because she's always whining about how she got a raw deal. Most people here, well, we don't really talk about stuff like that."

"Why not?"

"Because . . . because what's the point? We're here, and it is what it is, and it doesn't make any difference how we got here."

That made sense, I supposed.

"And I'd rather talk about something more . . . more important," he said.

"Like what?"

He fidgeted a bit, and examined his burger with more attention than it deserved. Could a demon blush? I could have sworn I saw a pink flush crawl over his face. He mumbled something I couldn't make out.

"What did you say?"

"Us. I want to talk about *us*."

"Us," I repeated stupidly.

"Yeah. You probably weren't paying much attention to what I told you when I picked you up. You were so completely freaked out."

I raised my eyebrows. "Can you blame me?"

"Not at all," he said quickly.

I did remember something he'd said several times. "I belong to you. That's what you told me."

He nodded rapidly. "Right."

"So that makes me—what? Your slave?"

His mouth fell open. I looked away so I could be spared

the sight of a chewed-up chunk of Quarter Pounder. He swallowed too quickly, and then started coughing.

"You okay?" I asked anxiously. I looked at the wall, where they usually post directions for the Heimlich maneuver.

He took a big gulp of his drink, and the coughing subsided. "Listen, I'm not like that," he said. "I absolutely do not believe that women should be subservient to men. When I was a little kid, my mother was into the women's-liberation movement. I was raised as a feminist."

"Well, that's . . . that's cool," I said. "So I'm not your slave. Then what am I?"

He lifted the scrap of roll that remained on his sandwich and scrutinized the cheese. "I told you before, I was next in line for a partner. You're supposed to be, you know, like, my mate. I mean, that's what it's called down here," he added hastily. "I think 'partner' is a nicer word." He gave me the crooked smile again. "Or maybe 'girlfriend.'"

I should have been shocked, but I wasn't. I think, way in the back of my mind, I'd known this all the time. He must have been relieved that I didn't cry out in horror, because he leaned forward and began to speak in a more confident—and confidential—way.

"You know, demons like me, we don't get any say in this matter. It's like a blind date, except you're stuck with the other person a whole lot longer. Not that I feel stuck," he said quickly. "I mean, when I saw you for the first time in that bedroom, all I could think was that I'd really lucked out."

He paused and looked at me anxiously, evidently waiting for some kind of reaction. I smiled weakly and nodded. Encouraged, he continued.

"I mean, you should see some of the chicks that are handed over to some of the other demons. Really ugly, and mean, or super pissed-off for being here, and they *stay* that way. Actually, to tell the truth, when I met you, I got a little nervous."

I managed to choke down a McNugget. "Why?"

He bit his lower lip and offered an abashed grin. "I could see you were kind of out of my league. I mean, you're obviously a pretty cool chick. You were in the popular crowd at school, right? Maybe you were even a cheerleader. I'll bet you went to lots of parties. And, like I said before, I was always kind of a nerd. A girl like you would never go out with a guy like me back . . . back in the real world. I hope you're not too disappointed."

Disappointment implied that there had been some sort of expectation on my part. I could honestly say that disappointment wasn't one of the feelings I was currently dealing with. "No, it's okay."

His eyes widened. "So you think we'll be good together?"

I felt like a hunk of reconstituted chicken was stuck in my throat. I took a long draw on my Coke. He was waiting for an answer.

"I don't know. I guess we'll have to wait and see."

I knew it wasn't the answer he'd been hoping for, but it didn't upset him. He actually seemed to relax a little. "That's cool. I mean, there's no rush. It's not like we're pressed for time or anything like that."

A slow but steady chill rose inside of me. I'm not stupid. I knew what he meant, I'd known all along, this wasn't fresh news. But to hear it like this. . . .

"Eternity," I said. "We're here forever."

"That's right." His forehead puckered. "You okay?"

"I want to go home," I whispered.

He wasn't alarmed. "Yeah, you must be wiped out. Let's go." Silently, I rose and followed him to the door. He continued to talk as we got into the car and took off. "Maybe you should go to sleep when we get home. Or maybe not. I picked you up at, what, midnight? And now it's, like, five o'clock. Maybe you should try to stay awake until ten, at least. Otherwise, it's going to be hard getting over the jet lag." He laughed. "I know it's not actually jet lag, but that's what we call it. There's no real word for it here. It's not like we're crossing actual time zones."

I could hear him talking as we drove, I could make out the words, and I knew what he was saying, but it was like a meaningless drone set against the beat of one word. *Eternity. Eternity. Eternity.*

More words. Always. Infinity. Forever and ever. World without end, amen. Bits and pieces of myths and religions and ohmigod ohmigod this is it, this is all there is. And all the while, Brad rambled on about jet lag and time zones. By the time we got back to the little house, all I wanted to do was run inside, crawl into bed, and escape in sleep.

But I knew I wouldn't be able to. Sleep, that is. I would just lie there, totally conscious and wide awake, and the words would keep on hammering in my head. Eternity, infinity, and so on. Distraction would be better.

"You gonna lie down now?" Brad asked.

"No, you're right, I should try to adjust to the time. We could watch some TV."

Brad picked up the remote. "Want to see what your mother's up to?"

"*No.*"

"How about your father?" he asked.

"He's dead."

"Oh, yeah, that was in your file," Brad said. "I'm sorry about that."

"Thank you," I replied automatically. "I never knew him; he died before I was born."

Brad nodded. "I know. Aren't you curious about him, though?"

"You mean, like, where he is now?"

"No, no, I mean what he was like *alive*. You want to see him?"

I was now distracted. "You can do that?"

"Sure! We've got a reality history channel. I watched the D-Day invasion from World War II the other day—the real one, not the movie. Just between us, the movie was better. When I was watching the actual battle, I didn't see any guy parachuting down and getting stuck in a tree. Of course, I don't know if that really happened—it might have been invented for the movie."

I had no idea what he was talking about, but I got the general idea. "Okay. I wouldn't mind seeing my father."

I settled down on the turquoise sofa while Brad began punching numbers into the remote. "Supposedly, with the next generation of sets, we're going to be able to key in specific dates," he said. "Right now, it's still pretty haphazard. You have to fiddle around a lot to get what you want."

"Can you fix it so it's before he married my mother?" I asked. "I'm not in the mood to look at her right now."

"I'll try."

As the screen came to life, I could see what looked like a government office. There was a big desk, flanked on either side by flags—the American one and the state flag, which looked like the Confederate flag from the Civil War. There was a framed portrait on the wall behind the desk. I recognized it immediately—President John F. Kennedy. So this had to be sometime in the early 1960s.

Brad sat down at the other end of the sofa. "I'll fast-forward till someone comes in," he said. Soon a busty woman with sculptured blond hair sped into the room, and Brad hit "play." The woman slowed down and placed the papers she was carrying on the desk. An old-fashioned phone with a dial rang, and she picked it up.

"Gooood mawnin', governor's office. How can Ah help you?"

I had to smile. I remembered those accents; I'd probably had one myself until the Eastern boarding schools crushed it.

"Thank you, I'll be sure to give him the message."

Just a few seconds later, there was the sound of a door opening, and the woman beamed. "Good morning, sir, how are you today?"

I leaned forward to get a good look at the man who had just entered the frame. Doing some rapid mental calculations, I figured he had to be in his mid-forties. He looked older, or maybe that was just how people looked back then in the days before workouts and serious skin care. He was kind of pudgy, with thinning hair combed over a bald spot, and a reddish face. I searched his face for any sort of genetic connection to myself. Maybe something around the earlobes. . . .

"Well, Ah tell ya, Betty Ann, Ah'd be a whole lot happier on the golf course, but here Ah am, and Ah reckon Ah'll stay awhile. Sugah, you want to fetch me a coffee?"

Betty Ann beamed. "Yes, sir, right away, sir."

Once she'd left, he picked up his phone and dialed. "Hey, Annie Sue, this here's the governor. Is the Speaker around? Thank you, sugah." And a moment later, "Jimmy, how ya doin'? Listen, Ah got a question for you. Is there a law says Ah gotta have a picture of that liberal sonofabitch on mah wall? Yeah, that's who Ah'm talkin' about, Mr. President John Fitzgerald Kennedy. Ah'm tellin' ya, pal, it's makin' me sick lookin' at him ev'ry mornin'. You really think he can be elected for a second term? Ain't there no way we can stop that from happening?"

I shouldn't have been shocked by what I was hearing. I'd heard and read enough about my father to know that Harley Hunsucker was so far to the right he could make George W. Bush look like a communist, so it was inevitable that he wouldn't be too crazy about JFK. But to hear him articulating what I knew was making me feel sick. Or maybe I was still thinking about eternity.

Brad broke in. "By the way, I don't think your father had anything to do with the assassination."

"But I'll bet he didn't shed any tears over it," I said.

When the telephone conversation was over, Harley Hunsucker accepted a coffee and a newspaper from the secretary. Once she'd left the room again, he put his feet on the desk, opened the newspaper, and disappeared behind it.

Brad hit a button, and another scene appeared on the screen. I recognized the school from the picture I'd seen in the magazine yesterday. And there he was, my dear daddy, with a fatter belly and a redder face, barring the door. Off on one side of the school, there were people holding signs demanding "Equal Rights Now." They were separated by police officers from the crowd on the other side of the school, who were yelling and screaming obscenities, including the dreaded "n" word.

A man holding the hand of a little girl approached the door. A couple of people with TV cameras moved in closer as Harley Hunsucker folded his arms and blocked the door. "Go away, folks. Jest move on down the road. We don't want any trouble."

The man nudged the little girl, who spoke in a clear, sweet voice. "I want to go to school."

My father crouched down so he was at her level. Clearly apprehensive, the poor kid took a step backward. At least my father had the decency not to yell, but the words were still pretty frightening.

"Well, that's just fine, little girl, fine and dandy, you want to get yourself some education, but you can't go to school here. This is a school for white children only. You'll jest have to get yer daddy to carry you on over to the colored school."

"Wow, what a jerk," Brad commented. "No offense."

"Are you kidding?" I shuddered. "I can't believe I'm related to this creep."

"Want me to fast-forward?"

"No, just shut it off." I couldn't even say I was upset. At this point in time, after the day I'd had, I was pretty much numb.

"At least he got what he deserved," Brad said.

"Is he here?" I asked.

"What?"

"Did he go to Hell when he died?"

"I don't know," Brad admitted. "What I meant was, he ended up with your mother. Hell on earth, right?"

I recalled Brad's explanation of my mother's deal with the devil. "That was part of the pact, wasn't it? He'd die, and she'd take over his job as lieutenant governor."

"Right. I hope watching this wasn't too depressing. You've been hit with a lot today."

I nodded and yawned simultaneously. "I'm exhausted." Then I wrinkled my nose. "Oh, jeez, I just realized, I don't have a toothbrush or anything to sleep in."

Brad shook his head and grinned proudly. "Hey, don't forget, I knew you'd be coming. There's a bag of stuff for you in the bathroom, and a whole drawer full of clothes."

"Great," I said. I got up, and Brad got up, too. And then I remembered something else.

"I guess . . . my clothes are in *your* bedroom."

Brad seemed to be looking just past me, and his cheeks went pink. "It's supposed to be *our* bedroom."

I swallowed. "Yeah. I know."

Brad still couldn't meet my eyes. "But, look . . . you've had a pretty traumatic day. You can stay in the guest room."

I'm sure he could see how relieved I was. "Okay, I will."

He finally looked at me and made an effort to smile. "And, uh, you can stay there for as long as you like. Until you feel ready . . . I mean, until you want to, you know—"

"I know, I get it," I said quickly. "Thanks, Brad."

Thanks? As I went down the hall to the bathroom, all I could think of was how stupid that sounded. Did I really need to thank him for not forcing me to sleep with him? On the other hand, from what I understood, he was entitled to me, so I guess he *was* doing me a favor.

It's not like I was a virgin. That milestone had been passed during the summer, when I was sent to a so-called leadership camp for the teen offspring of politicos. The only leadership skills I saw anyone develop were the kind that enabled you to facilitate access to beer and wine coolers. My little fling was with a guy named Robert, the son of a member of the Cabinet, and I wasn't in love with him. I think it was sheer boredom that drove us both into having our first real sexual adventure. If his father hadn't been someone fairly well known, I probably wouldn't even remember his last name.

So I wasn't hung up on saving myself. But I would have liked my next partner to be someone I cared about. Not a demon. And especially not a demon I'd just met.

Opening the toiletry bag in the bathroom, I was pleasantly surprised to see products I recognized. The brand of toothpaste that I preferred, the kind of deodorant I used, my favorite bath products—that was pretty thoughtful of him. When I came out, Brad had already gone into his room, and the door was closed. I went into the guest room and saw that he'd laid clothes on my bed. There were jeans, T-shirts, underwear. . . . I was too tired to look it all over, but some-where in the pile, I found a flannel nightgown printed with little pink flowers. At least Brad hadn't been expecting a sex goddess.

He was being kind, I thought as I curled up in bed and closed my eyes. Not demonic at all. Which made me wonder, as I drifted off to sleep—what could he possibly have done to deserve an eternity in Hell? Even if it was in one of the better neighborhoods. . . .

chapter
Seven

I WOKE UP to my first real morning in Hell. It hadn't been a bad night—my bed back in the dorm at Wood-bridge was lumpier. I couldn't remember if I'd dreamed, but I was sure I hadn't had any nightmares. Maybe people didn't have nightmares in Hell—a little compensation for actually existing in a nightmare.

Although I couldn't honestly say that I felt particularly tormented that morning. Whoever was responsible for the fake-time special effects was doing a good job. The light filtering through the gauzy curtains at the window actually felt like dim daylight.

I eased myself out of bed and padded out into the hallway. Brad's door was closed, so I went down to the bathroom and checked out the bathing facilities. I couldn't remember the last time I'd had a real shower, and I was feeling pretty grubby. This wasn't the greatest shower in the world. The pressure was weak, and I couldn't get the water as hot as I would have liked it to be. But I had the nice mango-scented bath gel that Brad had provided, and I got out of the shower feeling reasonably clean.

There was a mirror over the sink, and for the first time since I'd arrived, I took a good look at myself. I almost did a double-take. I'd forgotten about the short blond hair, the gold hoop on my right eyebrow, and the little sparkling gem on my left nostril. It was going to take me a while to get accustomed to this new look. And then I laughed out loud. Here I was thinking about getting used to a haircut when I had to get used to being dead. Well, at least I hadn't lost my famous sense of humor.

I noticed the Band-Aid on my right shoulder, and remembered the tattoo. I was pretty sure enough time had passed, and it probably didn't matter anymore anyway, so I pulled it off. He'd done a nice job, the tattoo artist. A blue-and-yellow butterfly. . . . It had been a good choice, even though I couldn't have known at the time that I'd be living in a place where I'd probably never see a real butterfly again.

I studied my image from a different viewpoint, and tried to ignore the superficial and decorative stuff. Did I *feel* different, being dead? What was "dead" supposed to feel like? It seemed to me that I was still a physical person, with physical needs. I wouldn't have slept if I hadn't needed sleep, the shower had refreshed me, all the usual bodily functions appeared to be in working order. The sensations were there. I forced an experimental cough, and it sounded real enough. I was breathing . . . and I thought maybe I was hungry.

A terry-cloth robe hung from a hook on the bathroom door. I put it on; it was scratchy, but the fit was okay. Once out in the hall, I followed a not-unpleasant scent to the kitchen.

Brad, in pajamas, stood at the stove with a long fork in his hand and pushed something around in a pan.

"Good morning," he said. "Do you like French toast?"

"Sure," I said. I couldn't take my eyes off the pajamas. They were printed with little pictures of wine bottles, cocktails, olives, and swizzle sticks, and phrases like "chin-chin" and "skoal," "bottoms up" and "cheers."

Brad noted the direction of my eyes and looked a little embarrassed. "We don't get much choice around here when it comes to clothes. At least they're comfortable."

I nodded. "Can I help?"

"No, everything's under control." He offered that cute apologetic smile that I was getting used to seeing. "It won't be the best you've ever had. There's only egg substitute, and the milk is the powdered kind. But I've got real maple syrup, straight from Vermont." He indicated the bottle on the table.

"How did you get it?"

"I had a job in Burlington."

"Doing what?"

"Usual stuff." He poked at the French toast with what seemed like unnecessary force. "I don't like to talk about work. Sit down."

I did as I was told. The little round table was set with plates and utensils and napkins. Nothing matched, but it was all where it was supposed to be.

Since I had almost always lived alone, you'd think I'd be accustomed to silence, but it felt uncomfortable when there was someone else in the room. "You said you're from Cincinnati, right?"

"Cleveland, actually. I went to university in Cincinnati. That's where I was before I came here."

"I've never been to Cincinnati. Or Cleveland."

"You haven't missed much."

Since I knew absolutely nothing about either city, I couldn't argue with that; so another potential topic of conversation was out. "What about your family?"

"What about them?"

"Are they still in Cleveland?"

"Yeah. Well, my older sister is married and living in the suburbs."

"How many sisters do you . . . *did* you have?"

"Three. One older, two younger."

"I was an only child," I told him.

"Yeah, I know."

It felt odd, him knowing so much more about me than I knew about him. But it seemed like I was not about to learn more today. Before I could ask another question, he turned away from the frying pan to me. "Look, um, I don't want to talk about the past. Okay?"

"Sure. I'm just trying to make conversation."

He brought the pan to the table and slid the slices of French toast onto our plates. Then he sat down and pushed the bottle of maple syrup toward me. "Go easy on that," he warned me. "I don't know when I'll be able to get my hands on another bottle."

"Aren't there many sinners in Vermont?" I asked. I cut off a chunk of French toast and took a tentative bite. It wasn't half bad.

"It's not that. It's just that . . . well, it's not exactly legal to bring stuff back here. I had to sneak it in under my cape. Like the products you've got in the bathroom. We can't get those brands here; I had to smuggle them in."

I recalled one of my classmates talking about the five luxury wristwatches from Switzerland she wasn't supposed to bring into the United States. "Is it like going through Customs at an airport?"

"Yeah, I guess, I wouldn't really know. You've probably been through more airports than I have."

I was eating steadily now—obviously, there was hunger in Hell—and had to chew and swallow before I could reply.

"Not the kind with Customs," I told him. "I don't even have a passport. I've never been out of the United States."

"*I've* never been out of Ohio," Brad said.

There was a moment of silence, and I suppose we were both thinking of all the places we'd never go to now. Brad worked on finishing off his French toast, but I could feel something distinctly like deep, dark depression creeping into the kitchen. Suddenly Brad stood up and interrupted the descent of the blues.

"Want to make like a tourist here? I could show you around."

I got up. "I'll go change."

In the pile of clothes still on my bed, I found everything I needed. Brad, or whoever picked out the clothes, had done his homework. Even the bra was my size. The quality of the clothes wasn't the best, and the color range was a little off-putting—violent fuchsia, a sickly pale green, a pink-and-blue bunny-printed T-shirt that was positively gag-worthy. It was all the stuff you'd find on the last day of a closeout sale at one of those big discount marts. But everything I tried on fit. Obviously, they'd been ready for me here.

Brad was waiting in the living room.

"I thought we could start out with a walk around the neighborhood," he said.

"Fine with me," I told him.

"Not that there's much to see," he warned me as we left the house. "There are no museums or galleries, or anything like that."

I was pretty sure he wasn't referring only to this neighborhood. "How about libraries?" I asked without much hope.

"None of those, either."

I supposed it all made sense. "Good artists and writers wouldn't go to Hell."

"Are you kidding?" Brad exclaimed. "There are plenty of

them here. Just because people have some kind of talent doesn't mean they can't be bad people. We got poets, musicians, ballerinas, you name it. It's funny, a lot of them are really shocked to find themselves here after they kick. Like, they think, because they're creative types, they didn't have to behave themselves when they were alive. There's this one guy, he dumped his wife and kids just so he could go hang out on a tropical island and paint. He had a great time, and he thought it would be cool because everyone loved his paintings. He's around here somewhere."

"So you've got all those rock stars who OD'd on drugs?"

"Some of them."

This was interesting. "Do they ever give concerts?"

"They're not supposed to," Brad said. "The powers-that-be aren't into providing pleasure to the general population. But sometimes people get together to play and the authorities look the other way."

"Couldn't artists get together and have underground exhibits? And writers could print out their work and distribute it. Are there Xerox machines?"

Brad grinned. "Hey, what are you, some kind of revolutionary? You just got here!"

"But is it possible?" I persisted. "Isn't there any flexibility in the rules? You just said sometimes authorities don't enforce them."

"That's true," Brad admitted.

"And it's not like all pleasure is forbidden," I went on. "Those McNuggets yesterday were okay. And that reality history channel could be cool, if you were watching someone like Benjamin Franklin. Or Elvis Presley."

I was afraid I might be coming off too pushy, but Brad just gave a noncommittal shrug. "I guess. I mean, it's all relative.

People think good and bad are absolutes, but it's not like that at all, and especially not here. Everything's negotiable. Of course, there's a lot of red tape, and everything has to go through all these crap committees, and it can take forever to get anything done, but eventually things happen."

"Who does the negotiations?" I asked. "Lawyers?"

He nodded. "Yeah, we got plenty of those."

"I guess Satan has the final say, right?"

"Depends. Most debates get resolved on a lower level."

"So Satan's like the Supreme Court?"

"Sort of." He frowned, and I thought for a minute I'd offended him or something, but he was looking past me. I turned and saw a woman running toward us, waving.

"Damn," he muttered. "It's Angie."

I recognized her—the neighbor we'd passed the day before.

"Brad, hi! Who's your friend?"

Brad made the introduction. "Angie, Jessica. Jessica, Angie."

The woman fixed her small green eyes on me. "So what are you in for?"

"Angie!" Brad exclaimed. "Most people don't like to talk about that."

Angie giggled. "Brad thinks I'm rude," she said.

"I was sold," I told her. "By my mother."

Angie's thin, arched eyebrows shot up. "Oh, wow!" And then her face fell. "Oh, damn." She turned to Brad. "Is she for you?"

Brad nodded, and Angie sighed, shifting her disappointed expression to me.

"All the good ones get matched up. You know what kind of guys I meet here? Losers."

Given where we were, that seemed perfectly logical to

me, but I tried to look sympathetic. Brad indicated a truck parked just ahead. "That looks like a moving van. Maybe we're getting a new neighbor."

Angie made a face. "With my luck, even if it's a guy, he died of natural causes." To me, she explained what she meant. "Really *old*. I was only thirty-five when I drowned in a motel swimming pool. Drunk, skinny-dipping at midnight . . . you get the picture."

There was a man on the sparse lawn directing the movers, but he looked too relaxed to be a new arrival. He was a slick-looking type, with hair that was just a little too perfectly groomed and patent-leather shiny. He wore an open-collar white shirt, and I could see a bunch of gold chains underneath.

Brad greeted him. "What's up, Tony?"

"Just getting the place ready for someone who's coming Wednesday." He glanced at the paper in his hand. "Alton Crenshaw."

The name rang a bell, and then I remembered. "So he's really going to be executed?"

"You know him?" Angie asked excitedly. "Is he cute?"

"Angie, he's a convicted murderer," Tony told her. "That's why he's being executed."

"So what?" Angie asked. "I'm a killer. As long as he's not one of those psycho serial types. Did he have a good reason?"

"He might be retarded," I told her, and then an image of handsome Sanders flashed across my mind, and I corrected myself. "Mentally challenged. A lot of people thought he shouldn't be executed, because he couldn't be held responsible for what he did."

Tony looked at his papers again. "Yeah, he's no mental giant, but he's not a complete yo-yo. According to this, he was smart enough to know he was committing a sin. But they gave him a break because he's got some brain damage, so he's coming here instead of one of the usual big-sin places. He's a friend of yours?"

I shook my head. "No, I only heard about him."

"Jessica just arrived yesterday," Brad explained. "I picked her up."

"She's for you?" Tony whistled and leered at me. "Not bad, pal. She looks like she knows her way around a guy."

"C'mon, Jessica, let's go," Brad muttered. We left Angie behind with Tony, and moved on. "Sorry about that. Tony's been here since sometime in the fifties; he doesn't know how to talk to females. You know, the old sexist mentality."

"Is he a demon, too?"

"Nah, just a resident."

We were at a corner now. "Which way?" I asked.

"You choose."

I looked both ways. "Does it make any difference?" The roads to the right, to the left, and straight ahead all looked identical.

"Not really," Brad admitted. "There's a strip mall down that way, with some shops, like a hardware store and a grocery store. That's where you get the fake eggs and the fake milk, stuff like that. We could take the car later and check out some other areas farther out. But this is as good as it gets around here. Sorry."

"For what?"

"Well, I'm supposed to be showing you the sights. But there aren't any. At least, not any you'd want to see."

I had to smile. "It's not your fault. You're not in charge here."

"No," he said.

I looked at him thoughtfully. "But you're not a nobody, either. You're not just a regular resident, you're a demon."

He gave a little shrug, which I assumed was an assent.

I pressed on. "How did that come about? Were you made a demon when you arrived? Or was it some kind of promotion? Did you have to work your way up to it?"

"It's like any business—it's who you know. I met a demon from Toledo, we played cards, I let him win, and he recommended me."

"To Satan?"

"Hey, I'm not *that* connected. No, he knew someone in Human Resources. Then I took a test, to show I wasn't an idiot. And I had to do an internship under observation, to prove I wasn't going to try to stay on earth when I went back for jobs."

I stopped. "You can do that? Run away from Hell and get back to earth for good?"

"No," he replied quickly. "But people try."

"Are you ever . . . tempted? To stay on earth?"

"*No*," he said, more forcibly this time. "I belong here. This is home."

I didn't know what to say about that, so I changed the subject. "Alton Crenshaw—would that have been a Supreme Court decision?"

"Who?"

"Alton Crenshaw, the convicted murderer who was maybe borderline mentally challenged. Was it Satan who decided he should come here instead of one of the crummier neighborhoods?"

"I don't know. It's possible, I guess."

"Have you ever met him?"

"Satan? No." Brad looked at me curiously. "How come you're always asking about him?"

"Because . . . I don't know . . . because he just seems interesting." I knew that sounded lame, and I could tell Brad thought so, too. I decided to confess.

"I guess I've always had kind of a little crush on him."

Amusement and disbelief fought for control of Brad's expression. "Are you serious? You've got a crush on Satan?"

"It's just a fantasy thing," I added hastily. "Or maybe I should call it a literary thing. And I'm not the only one. We read *Paradise Lost* last year, and half my English class felt the same way."

Now Brad looked blank. "What's *Paradise Lost*?"

I wasn't shocked. If Brad had been a computer geek, he was a science-and-technology guy and probably didn't take many English courses. And it's not like *Paradise Lost* was on any recent best-seller lists.

"It's this really long poem by John Milton. It was written back in the seventeenth century, I think, and it was about Adam and Eve getting thrown out of the Garden of Eden. Satan's one of the main characters. Actually, a lot of people think he's the hero."

Brad was taken aback. "You gotta be kidding me. The so-called biggest bad guy in the universe is the hero of a poem?" He started laughing.

"What's so funny?"

"Well, like I said, I never met him. But I know someone who knows a guy who worked for him. And you know what he says? Satan's just another big dumb fat cat with a lot of smart henchmen who do all the dirty work. He watches football and old John Wayne Westerns all day on an illegal cable-from-earth hookup, he drinks bootleg whiskey and smokes huge smelly cigars some demon picks up for him in Cuba. And he's got some serious BO."

Now I was shocked. "You're kidding."

"That's what I've heard. Could be an exaggeration, I guess. I know he cleans up for public appearances."

"He shows up in public?"

"Only for major events. Like when some really important political figure arrives, he might welcome him personally in a ceremony. The rest of the time, he's a couch potato."

I digested this. "Wow. That's so not *Paradise Lost*. Milton portrays him very sympathetically. In the story, Satan's a fallen angel. He's a rebel, he's ambitious, and he doesn't like the fact that there's this one big authority figure in Heaven who's in charge of everything. He's angry and proud, and kind of romantic, like Heathcliff."

"Who?"

"From *Wuthering Heights*. It's another book."

"I was never much of a reader," Brad admitted.

I thought about the pathetic handful of books back in his house, and the fact that there were no libraries in Hell. "I'm going to miss reading."

"I miss my games," Brad said. "Ms. Pac-Man. Super Mario Brothers. Are they still around?"

"I've heard of them," I replied. "They're video games, aren't they?"

He sighed. "I've seen some of the new stuff on TV. Nintendo, Game Boy, PlayStation, all those great gadgets and accessories—they must be pretty cool."

"The girl next door to me in my dorm had an Xbox," I told him.

"Wow, lucky you."

"I never played," I admitted. "I wasn't into computer games."

"I guess we don't have all that much in common," Brad said, and there was a wistful note in his voice. I looked at him, and I was struck by the sad-little-boy expression on his face. I wasn't sure if he was jealous of my crush on Satan or if he just wished we'd been better matched. I couldn't help feeling sorry for him, and I wanted to say something nice.

"Actually, we have more in common than you think," I said.

"Like what?"

"You said you thought I must have been very cool back at school. Well, I wasn't. I was quiet, and I pretty much kept to myself. I definitely wasn't popular. The reason I never played Xbox with my neighbor is because she never invited me."

He was surprised. "You're kidding."

I shook my head. "I didn't even look like this on earth—well, not for very long. I'm sure a lot of my classmates considered me a nerd. I would never have been a cheerleader or prom queen or anything like that."

"Really?"

"Yeah." I remembered his comment yesterday at McDonald's, and mimicked it. "Hope you're not too disappointed."

He shook his head vigorously. "Not at all. It's better like this! We're not so different. I don't feel so . . . so beneath you."

I disagreed. On a pre-Hell, earthly social level, we might have been on the same level. Not anymore. He'd been sent to Hell because he'd committed some sort of real transgression, whereas I was an innocent victim of my mother's evil ambition. He was kind now, but he must have been bad on earth. I'd been good. Not great, maybe. But I hadn't done anything terrible, illegal, or immoral. He was a sinner, I wasn't.

But I didn't say anything. Brad was actually looking more at ease now, more genuinely relaxed, and, whatever terrible things he'd done on earth, he was being nice with me.

It was interesting, though, to learn that even the devil's flunkies could be intimidated by a cheerleader.

Chapter Eight

LOOKING BACK, I can honestly say that it didn't take too long for me to get a solid fix on Hell. Within a week, I had a pretty good sense of what it was all about.

Not much. Certainly not what I could have ever imagined.

When I was a kid, I had recurring nightmares about a story I read in a collection of Hans Christian Andersen fairy tales. I even remember the title of the story—"The Girl Who Trod on the Loaf." I can't recall the details, but it was about some nasty, proud little girl adopted by rich people who was given a loaf of bread to take to her poor mother. On her way to her mother's, she encountered a pool of mud. She didn't want to step into it and get her fancy shoes dirty, so she put the loaf in the mud to use as a stepping stone to cross the pool, but when she stepped on it, she sank, and ended up in Hell. I remember that version of Hell vividly; there was even an illustration—slimy toads, snakes crawling over her, spiders building webs on her, images that fueled my dreams for many nights. I'd seen nothing like that here—so far, my Hell was pest-free, which was more than I could say about my dorm room back at Woodbridge. In fact, come to think of it, I hadn't seen any forms of nonhuman life in Hell. I supposed bugs and other animals couldn't be held responsible for their nastier actions.

I'd never read Dante's *Inferno*, but I knew about it from a Web site that had been popular at the school I went to before Woodbridge. You could take a multiple-choice test online and find out which of Dante's circles of Hell you would probably end up in when you died. According to Dante, there were nine circles, with each circle representing a different sin, like lust, or gluttony, and the Hell you went to was based on the type of sin you'd committed.

As far as I could tell, real Hell didn't appear to be that segregated or well organized. My own neighborhood was a mishmash, a regular melting pot of sins. For example, Angie next door—I learned that she was your basic lust sinner. She killed her husband when she found out he was having an affair with another woman. It was totally a passion thing, he didn't even have a good insurance policy. And I found out why Tony, the guy who'd been setting up Alton Crenshaw's home, had been sent here. In life, he'd been a con man, a regular rip-off artist, who sold nonexistent plots of land to people, and I suppose that would come under the category of fraud. The guy across the street had been a gang leader, so I'm guessing he'd have been labeled violent. All these people would have been in separate circles in Dante's Hell, but they were all living in the same community here.

I learned about these people from Angie—Brad didn't like talking about anyone's past. I still didn't know why *he* was here.

I found out about a couple of things we had in common, though. We both had occasional massive cravings for spicy chicken wings. You could get buckets of them here, just like on earth. You might be wondering why something so tasty would be available in Hell, but you had to consider the side effects, which were also the same as the ones I'd had on earth. I'd eat way too many wings, and then I'd feel totally queasy and disgusting, and want nothing more than a week of fresh fruit and vegetables. Only, in Hell, you couldn't *get* any fresh fruit or vegetables, so the sick feeling stayed with you a whole lot longer. That was the difference.

I discovered another obsession we shared when I came out of the bathroom one evening after a brief, lukewarm bath (I could never get the water hot enough to enjoy a long soak). Brad was glued to the TV with a look of rapture on his face.

"What are you watching?" I asked him.

He turned to me with a sheepish grin, and for one icky moment I thought I might have caught him spying on some bedroom activity somewhere.

"You'll probably think this is really stupid," he said. "But I saw this flick when I was a kid, and I was crazy about it. I even bought the album."

I'm sure my wide eyes must have given away my response before I even spoke. Squealed, actually. There, before my very eyes, were John Travolta and his pals dancing on the bleachers and singing, "Tell me more, tell me more . . ."

"*Grease*! Ohmigod, it's my all-time favorite movie!"

"You're kidding! I saw it, like, at least thirty years ago! It's still popular?"

I nodded fervently. "At my last school, before Woodbridge, there was a girl on my hall who had the DVD." I stopped. "DVDs are what we have now instead of videos."

Brad rolled his eyes. "Jessica, I watch people watching TV all the time. I *know* what DVDs are."

"Right, of course. Anyway, this girl, she watched *Grease* practically every Saturday night, and if she liked you, she let you come in her room and watch it with her. And she'd leave her door open, so anyone else could watch from out in the hall."

Brad grinned. "Where were you, in or out?"

I smiled back. "Guess." I could still see myself, on tiptoe, trying to peek over the shoulders of the other outsiders in front of me.

Once again, I could see that he was pleased to know that I hadn't been one of the queen bees. His eyes were warm, and for the first time I noticed a golden glimmer in the deep-brown color.

I looked away and focused on the screen. "How did you get this? They don't have video stores in Hell, do they?"

"I was surfing and just came across someone watching it on TV. And I fiddled with the controls and got their TV screen to fill *our* screen. So we don't have to watch the other people watching the movie."

Our screen. This probably wasn't the first time he'd used that particular first-person plural possessive pronoun around me, but it was the first time I really heard it. It gave me a funny feeling. I was still staying in the guest room, but I was beginning to come to grips with the fact that I wasn't a visitor in this house. *Our* house?

I glanced at Brad, but I didn't think he'd picked up on his grammatical usage. He was glued to the pretty, skinny, sweet-faced blonde in the nightgown, standing on a porch and singing about how she was hopelessly devoted. I had to smile. Even in my limited experience with fellow teens of the male species, I knew that they all lusted after this vision of Olivia Newton-John. Personally, I couldn't understand the appeal—she was so prissy and uptight-looking. I guess it was a guy thing. Fortunately, I couldn't imagine any red-blooded girl getting jealous over this—the actress was way out of any normal guy's league (even if she had to be practically ancient by now). I smoothed a wrinkle in my own very similar floral nightgown. I was a blonde, too, but that was where the similarities ended—Olivia Newton-John had no tattoos or piercings.

Once again, my own mental ramblings made me feel weird. Was I actually comparing my situation, right now, right here, with that of some regular girl watching TV with her boyfriend?

I concentrated on the movie to keep my imagination under control. As usual, just as on those Saturday nights back at school, I got completely caught up in it. Brad did, too. And by the end of the movie, we were both getting silly, singing, "You're the one that I want, ooh, ooh, ooh. . . ." We even took the positions of the actors, holding hands and beaming at each other.

Then the credits began to roll. Immediately we dropped each other's hands.

"Well," I said, "that was fun."

Brad's grin was huge. "Yeah. You know, I'm going to see if I can get my hands on cables and stuff next time I'm on earth. Maybe I could fix up some kind of recording mechanism that would work on this TV. We could tape movies and have them to watch whenever we want. Wouldn't that be cool?"

I nodded. "I guess, if I have to be stuck in Hell, I should be grateful that I'm stuck with a techie."

His grin faded. Had I hurt his feelings? I really needed to learn to think before I spoke.

I got up. "Guess I'll go to bed now."

"G'night," he said.

I really hoped I hadn't hurt his feelings.

Chapter
Nine

I KNEW we had neighbors on the other side of our house, because I'd heard raised voices arguing late at night, but I didn't meet them until the next day. One of them, a very shriveled, really old guy, was sitting on his front steps, and he waved to me as I passed.

"Hey, cutie! Wanna spend some time with an old fart?"

I had to smile. It was an unusual come-on line, and I was up for some entertainment. I introduced myself. "I'm Jessica Hunsucker. I'm new here."

"Welcome to the neighborhood, Jessie," the old guy said. "We're always happy to see a doll like you." He offered a toothless grin. "Even though you're not my type." He held out a grizzled hand, and I gave it a brief shake.

"And you are . . . ?" I inquired politely.

"You ever heard of Clyde Barrow?"

The name rang a bell, and then I gasped. I'd seen the old movie on TV ages ago. Warren Beatty and Faye Dunaway played the real-life legendary hoodlums. "You mean, from *Bonnie and Clyde*? Who robbed banks and killed people in the 1930s?" I frowned, remembering the end of the movie, when the two of them had been shot down and killed in slow motion by police. They couldn't have been more than twenty-five when they died.

"*You're* Clyde Barrow?"

"Well, no, not exactly," he said. "But I *knew* him. I was in the gang. My name's Joe Flicker. Ever heard of me?"

"No. Sorry."

He grimaced. "Yeah, it was the good-looking ones that got all the publicity. No one ever took *my* picture. But I was there, honey, right by Clyde's side. And they never got me, I died of natural old age. Always knew I'd end up here, too. Back when I was a drinking man, I used to make a toast." He held up an imaginary bottle. "Here's to Hell. May the stay there be as pleasant as the way there."

"Is it?" I asked.

"It ain't bad. Made a friend."

As if he'd been cued to make an entrance, another man came out the door. This one was about the same age, maybe a little younger. He didn't look as friendly as Joe Flicker, though. His lips were thin and pressed together tightly, and his eyes were mean.

"What do you want?" he barked at me.

Joe introduced us. "Howard, Jessie. She's new, she wants to meet people."

Howard's face registered suspicion. "Why?"

I explained, "Just because . . . well, if you're new to a place, it's nice to know something about your neighbors."

"What do you want to know?" he asked, in a tone that made it clear he wasn't interested in telling me anything about himself.

"Like, for example . . . why you're here. I understand about Mr. Flicker—he told me what he used to do."

"Call me Joe," the old man said.

"Well, don't ask *me* why I'm here," the other man snapped. "Because I don't have the slightest idea. *I* never robbed any banks."

Joe Flicker let out a cackle. "I'll tell you why you're here, you old coot. Because you were a mean old SOB." He turned to me. "Treated his kids like dirt. Wife, too."

"She deserved it. She was a tramp. And the kids were worthless."

Joe snorted. "Face it, pal. You just weren't meant to have a wife and a family—you were miserable. So you took it out on them. You had to come here to find out who you were." He explained to me. "We're partners." He winked. "If you know what I mean."

I nodded. "Okay. That's cool."

But the other guy wasn't too thrilled with Joe's announcement. "You don't have to tell the world."

Joe gave another cackle. "There ain't no closets in Hell, Howard. Too bad we couldn't have come out when we were alive. We might have been nicer people."

"Speak for yourself," the other one growled.

Another question came to me. "Joe, if you killed a lot of people in cold blood just for money, how come you're here, in this neighborhood?"

Now it was Joe's turn to look embarrassed. "Long story."

"No, it's not," Howard retorted. "It's because you didn't kill anyone. You just tagged after Clyde like a little pet poodle. You never drew your gun, you were scared out of your chicken mind!"

"That ain't true," Joe exclaimed angrily. He got to his feet. "You take that back, you old piece of shit!"

"Still can't deal with it, huh?" Howard taunted. "Won't

admit you had a thing for that young buck. Talk about hiding in a closet!"

Their voices were rising, and I could see that a battle was brewing. I beat a hasty retreat.

I told Brad about meeting Joe Flicker and Howard when he came home from work that evening.

"Now, let me get this straight," I said, as I set the kitchen table with the chipped and mismatched plates. "They're not in Hell because they're gay, are they?"

"No, no," Brad assured me. "Being gay has no sin value. Sexual orientation doesn't count for anything down here."

I was pleased to hear that. It confirmed what I already believed. "Well, that's a relief. The way some people back on earth talk, you'd think gay people were evil incarnate."

"Yeah, people can get these nutty notions," Brad said. "I heard that, back in the Middle Ages, some people thought you went to Hell if you were left-handed." He sniffed. "I smell something burning."

So did I, and I dashed to the oven. "Oh, no!" I wailed. The pizza I'd picked up earlier and put in the oven to warm was now black. "This is impossible! I just put it in, like, two minutes ago!"

Brad grimaced. "I'm sorry, I should have told you. None of this equipment works very well. Look." He opened the freezer compartment of the refrigerator and withdrew an ice-cube tray. Taking it to the sink, he held it upside down, and water poured out. "I put this in the freezer a week ago."

I should have guessed the stove would be out of order. I still wasn't *completely* acclimated to the ways of Hell.

"Why were you doing this anyway?" Brad asked, looking at the blackened remains on the baking tray. "We could go out for pizza."

"We've been going out every night since I got here," I

reminded him. "I thought it would be nice to have dinner at home."

He looked pleased. "Just the two of us, huh?"

To be honest, I'd been thinking more about the fact that our kitchen didn't have that greasy fast-food smell of the restaurants we'd been frequenting. But he could be right. I might have been thinking about dinner-for-two in a remotely romantic way. Subconsciously, of course. Oh, I don't know, maybe consciously. Brad was growing on me. And I still knew so little about him. . . .

With the ruined pizza, it didn't look like an intimate dinner at home would happen, since there was absolutely nothing else to eat in the house. But Brad surprised me.

He opened a cabinet, pushed some dented pots and pans aside, and pulled out a large can. "I've been saving this," he said.

I examined the can. The words on the label were all in French, and I'd only started French a month before coming to Hell, but I recognized the word for "duck."

"Wow. Did you set up a temptation in France?"

"No." I got another one of those cute abashed grins, the ones that said, *I'm just a little bit ashamed of myself.* They'd become kind of endearing. I knew a confession was coming.

"I stole it," he admitted. "I was setting something up in New York. This creepy professor at some university, he'd invited this really naïve freshman girl to his apartment for dinner. He was going to put this fancy duck stew in a pot and pretend he'd made it himself to impress her."

I was taken aback. "That's a sin? Pretending you cooked something you actually bought?"

"No, the temptation to sin would come later." Now he seemed more than a little bit ashamed. "He was going to give her wine, and she'd never drunk anything alcoholic before, and . . ." His voice drifted off.

"He was going to seduce her?"

"Not rape her or anything like that," he said quickly. "Just get her in the mood to say yes."

I didn't say anything, and his eyes darkened. "Look, it's my job, I have to set up the temptations. It's not my decision whether the jerk follows through or not!"

"I'm not blaming you," I said quickly. "I was just curious. What happened?"

"I didn't stick around long enough to find out. All I could do was grab the duck stuff so he couldn't impress her with his fake cooking. I took something else, too." He went back to the cabinet and brought out a bottle of red wine. "At least she'd be able to stay sober and say no to the asshole."

I smiled. He really was so sweet.

"And that's when I asked to be transferred to Finance," he added. "Helping people rip each other off isn't as depressing."

"I understand," I said.

Brad sighed, and stared into space for a moment. Then he opened the can of duck stew. I put the stew in a pot, turned on a burner, and watched it very carefully. I wanted us to have a nice dinner. Maybe even have a little wine with it.

chapter
Ten

BRAD TRIED to entertain me when he wasn't working. He took me out in the car one day, and pointed out some areas that looked like high-rise housing projects, city dumps, and a massive landfill that absolutely reeked, but nothing worse.

I walked to the little strip mall Brad had pointed out. I'd been wondering about money in Hell, what kind of currency was used here, but Brad told me there wasn't any money, you just took what you wanted. Unfortunately, there was nothing that anyone would want. I went into what looked like an antique store. There were chipped china figurines of women in old-fashioned clothes, costume jewelry with missing stones, some rusty unmatched silverware, plain glass ashtrays—it was like a really bad flea market.

The place was empty, and the old woman at the counter seemed pleased to have company. "Can I help you?"

"You don't happen to have anything to read, do you?" I asked her.

She smiled in a shifty way and lowered her voice, which didn't make any sense, since there was no one else around. "What did you have in mind?"

"Well, books, I guess. Or magazines."

She rubbed her hands together in a crafty manner. "You like magazines, huh?" Her knees creaked as she crouched down and opened a drawer behind the counter. "Take a look at this." Her eyes darted back and forth, as if to make sure no one was watching, and then she slapped the magazine on the counter.

It was *People*, and since I didn't recognize the person on the cover, I knew it had to be pretty old.

"'Sexiest Man Alive' issue," the woman said reverently. She opened it to reveal a photo of someone I'd never heard of with truly awful hair. "He's dead now. Not here, though. Too bad, huh?"

"Too bad," I echoed.

"This is strictly black-market goods," the woman informed me. "You want it, you gotta give me something of equal value."

"Like what?"

"Chocolate," she said. "And not the crap you get here. I'm talking the real thing, dark, with almonds." She appraised me. "You don't look like a sinner, even with those nasty piercings. I'll bet you were sold, and that means you've got a demon mate." She raised her eyes to the ceiling. "He ever go there? He could get his hands on some good stuff."

"I'll see what I can do," I said politely. But since I'd only read *People* magazines in waiting rooms, I didn't see any reason to knock myself out getting my hands on ancient copies now. And I could think of a lot of other stuff I'd rather Brad smuggle down here.

Anyway, by the end of my second week, all of my preconceived notions of Hell were shot to you-know-where. Hell was not hot; the average weather conditions were gray and cloudy, with an occasional glimpse of sun that reminded you of the kind of days you'd never see again. In other words, gloomy, but not physically painful. I hadn't noticed anyone suffering from excessive thirst or hunger. There was water, and the usual soft drinks you could find in any fast-food restaurant, but nothing fresh like juices, and you could forget about smoothies.

I hadn't seen anyone in chains, or weeping uncontrollably, or pushing boulders up mountains only to have them roll back down. No lakes of fire, no rivers of blood.

There was only one word that could adequately describe the Hell in which I lived: boring. Actually, that wasn't the only word—even without a thesaurus at hand, I could come up with a few more. Tedious, monotonous, dull, dull, dull. Day after day of the same old same-old. For people who had jobs, like Brad, there was at least some variation to each day. But for me, there was little I could do to break up the routine. True, I could vary my meals—there were half a dozen fast-food joints to choose from, or I could shop for prepared frozen dinners that looked different (but essentially tasted the same). I could take different routes on my daily walk, but I'd only pass houses and yards that were almost identical, no matter which direction I took.

Yesterday, I ran into Angie, the neighbor, and she invited me into her house for a coffee.

"I don't see you around that much when I take my walks," I told her. "What do you do all day?"

"I work part-time," Angie told me. "I'm a hairdresser."

"How did you get that job?"

"That's what I was before. I worked in a full-service salon. Hair, nails, waxing, all the treatments. Of course, there's not much call for that kind of thing here."

I thought I understood. "People don't care how they look?"

"Oh, no, it's not that at all. Didn't Brad tell you? We all stay the same. Like, we don't get older, or fatter, or anything like that. And our hair doesn't grow, so it doesn't need cutting. Nails don't grow, either. And if you waxed just before you came, you'll never have to do that again."

I'd never had my legs waxed—it seemed like a lot of unnecessary pain. Of course, if what Angie said was true, I could just shave my legs right now and the hair wouldn't grow back. My legs wouldn't be as smooth as they'd be if I went to Angie for a waxing, though. But did I care? And something else—would Brad care? Hastily, I shoved that thought aside. I wasn't ready to start considering questions like this. Not yet.

Angie was still talking. "So I get a few people who want to change their color or their style, but there aren't enough to keep me in full-time work. I'm not the only hairdresser here."

I had begun to realize that all sorts of former professions were found in Hell. Lawyers, of course, but doctors, too, the kind who did unnecessary surgeries just to make more money. And there seemed to be a lot of people who'd worked in city public-service jobs, like the post office or the department of motor vehicles, those offices where people always looked so mean and told you you'd been standing in the wrong line for the past forty-five minutes.

I asked Brad about the possibility of getting a job here, but he wasn't optimistic. I was only sixteen, I didn't have any skills or experience, and besides, the real sinners had dibs on the jobs. It was very confusing to me—I couldn't tell whether the worst sinners were being punished or rewarded. In any case, people like me, who hadn't earned their way here, were low on the status pole and destined for eternal unemployment.

I tried not to whine about my boredom, but occasionally the little complaint would slip out. Though Brad was sympathetic, there wasn't much he could do about it. Occasionally, he'd smuggle in a book or magazine for me to read, which was very sweet of him, especially because he suffered for it. I'd leap onto any reading material and devour it in solitude, leaving him with no one to talk to. He expected more from me, and he deserved more, too. He was so kind, and he made no demands; the least I could do was provide him with some companionship.

And it wasn't like hanging with Brad was a hardship. Sometimes I wondered, if we'd been on earth in the same place at the same time, and still around the same ages, whether we might have hooked up. Not that I'd fallen madly in love with him or anything like that. But there was definitely some sort of connection happening. And becoming more like . . . I don't know. Something.

My favorite time of day was when he came home from work and told me stories about life back on earth. He might not have finished his college education, but he was smart, he had a good sense of humor, and he was easy to be with. I wouldn't say I'd accepted what had happened to me, or that I had resigned myself to the notion of eternity in Hell—but at least Brad was good company. I wanted to be good company for him.

On that particular day, though, the two-week anniversary of my arrival, he came home and I could see immediately that he wasn't in a very good mood.

"Rough day?" I asked.

He nodded.

"Want to talk about it?"

"Not really. Here, I brought you a newspaper."

"Thanks."

He slumped down in a chair and picked up the remote. I curled up on the sofa with my newspaper. Every now and then, I glanced over in his direction. He was staring at the TV screen, but I could tell he wasn't watching it.

By now, I'd learned that his job could get to him. Usually, he laughed it off or joked about it, but sometimes it bugged him, how easily people could be tempted to do really nasty things. He looked seriously down today, and he needed attention. At least I could try to entertain him, and I put the newspaper down.

"I thought of something today," I told him. He didn't turn down the TV but he looked in my direction. I took that as a sign of encouragement and continued. "I was surfing with the remote, and I found a library. People were sitting around and reading, and I was wondering, would it be possible to photograph the pages? And print them out? Then I could put the pages together and have whole books to read! What do you think? Could that be done with the equipment you've got here?"

"Yeah, I guess it's possible," he said, but there was a notable lack of enthusiasm in his voice. Despite that, I went on.

"Then I surfed some more, and somehow I managed to hit on a classroom in a university somewhere. It was a really boring class—geology, I think—but it gave me an idea. If I could find an interesting course, I could take it! I mean, I know I couldn't enroll or get credits, but I could sort of unofficially audit the course. You could help me figure out how to access it every day, and I could learn something new. Like a language, maybe. I always wanted to speak Italian."

His eyes were dull, and I couldn't tell if he was really listening, but I kept going. "And I figured, there's got to be some dead Italian sinners down here somewhere, right? I could get a conversation group going, we could meet once a week. Wouldn't that be neat?"

He shrugged, and I couldn't detect even the slightest hint of interest in his expression, but still I didn't give up. "And then it occurred to me, if I could get into libraries and class-rooms, I could get into museums, and art galleries, and all sorts of places. I could follow a tour through some foreign country, and it would be almost like traveling! We could go to Italy together!"

His eyes seemed to darken.

"Or France," I added. "Anywhere!" I was speaking louder so I'd be heard over the TV noise, but he still didn't respond. "Could you turn the sound down?" I asked him.

"You sure you want me to do that?" he asked. "There might be a book popping up on the screen, and you'll want to copy it."

Somehow, I didn't catch the edge in his voice. "Well, it wouldn't make any difference if the sound was off— it's not like the book would be talking. . . ." My voice trailed off as I realized there was significant annoyance written all over his face.

"What are you trying to do?" he demanded to know.

It was annoyance bordering on anger. I was completely taken aback. "I'm just thinking about things I could do here. Things *we* could do."

"Things to make life here more pleasant?" His voice rose. "More *fun*?"

"Well . . . yeah. What's wrong with that?"

He stood up. "Jessica, we're in Hell! We're not supposed to be having fun!"

"But . . . but I'm bored, and—"

He wouldn't let me finish. "You're supposed to be bored!" he yelled. "That's the point! Hell is boring, haven't you figured that out yet? You're not supposed to be enjoying yourself, you're supposed to suffer!"

Now I was annoyed, and my own voice rose. "Why should I have to suffer? I never did anything wrong!"

"Yeah, well, you had bad luck," he snapped. "You're just going to have to deal with it, okay?"

"No, not okay," I shot back. "Brad, what's the matter with you? Are you actually telling me you don't want life to be better?"

"No, I don't!" He put both hands to his head, as if he'd just been struck by a massive headache. "Jessica, I did something wrong, I'm supposed to suffer! People died because of me! I have to pay for my sins!" Then, to my astonishment, his hands moved from the sides of his head to cover his face, and I thought he might be crying.

Having been alone and a loner for most of my life, I'd never been in a situation like this before, and I wasn't sure what to do. I wanted to comfort him, but I didn't know how. So I operated on instinct—I moved closer and touched his shoulder. He looked away, but at least he didn't push me aside, so I stayed where I was and left my hand where it was.

Finally, he took his hands from his face and sat down heavily on the sofa. I sat at the other end and spoke softly. "Brad?"

"Hm?"

"What did you do?"

There was a moment of silence, and then he spoke. "I told you, I was into computers."

"Yes."

"I was a hacker."

"You broke into computer systems?"

"Yeah. It was just for kicks, all my nerdy pals were doing it. We fooled around with stupid stuff at the university. Moving data around, changing grades. I put a whole fraternity on probation."

"And that's what sent you to Hell?"

"No." He took a deep breath. "I had a part-time job over at the university hospital. Making pharmacy deliveries to the wards. I had a boss, this pharmacist who was a real jerk, a total ass—he was always on my case, barking at me, telling me I did everything wrong. So . . . I wanted to make him look like an idiot. I figured out how to hack into the pharmacy's system, and I changed a bunch of prescriptions. I figured one of the doctors or nurses would catch the mistake, and my boss would be fired for putting patients in danger. Only . . . only nobody noticed the mistakes. And five patients died because they got the wrong medication."

I could hear the pain he was feeling in his voice. "Oh, Brad . . . that's awful. I can't imagine how you must have felt."

"It was my fault that they died," he said.

"But you didn't mean for them to die," I said. "It was a terrible accident. You weren't trying to kill them."

"But I did," he said flatly.

I couldn't argue with that. So now I knew why Brad was in Hell. Five dead people—that was pretty bad. Even so, I was still confused. What Brad had done was careless and stupid, that was for sure, and it had tragic consequences. But was it enough to send a person to Hell?

I needed more information. "Then, if someone has too much to drink and drives a car, and kills someone in an accident, does that mean the driver will go to Hell when he dies?"

"Not necessarily," Brad said. "Not if the driver felt sincerely bad about what he did, and repented, or tried to make up for it in some way. And if he quit drinking, so it wouldn't happen again."

"But you just kept on hacking and didn't repent?"

"No. I didn't have time to repent." He sighed. "The same day those people died, I was killed in a car accident." He paused, and offered me a sad little smile. "I was hit by a drunk driver."

I flinched. "Who won't go to Hell because he'll repent."

"Probably," Brad acknowledged.

There was a lot to absorb. But one thing I was already certain about. "It's not fair," I stated firmly. "If you'd lived, I'm sure you would have felt awful about those people. You *do* feel terrible, you're repenting right now. Doesn't that count for something?"

"No. Once you're here, you're here."

"But it's not *right*!" I exclaimed. "Okay, maybe it was your fault that the five people died, but it's not your fault that you couldn't try to make up for it. You didn't get a chance! It's just not fair."

He touched my hair. "Didn't anyone ever tell you life isn't fair, Jessica? Well, neither is death."

He was right, of course. A person only had to watch a news program or read a paper to know that all over the world people were suffering and dying through no fault of their own. Criminals could get rich while honest people stayed poor. Nasty people could get all the breaks while bad things happened to good people. Children were hungry, people got sick. There was no logic, no justice. Nothing made sense on earth. Why should it be any different in Hell? I moved closer to Brad, and he put an arm around me.

"I've never talked about any of this before," he said. "You're the first."

"Does it feel better to talk about it?" I asked him.

"I don't feel so . . . alone."

"Because you're not." I sighed. "We're in this together." My tone was more resigned than enthusiastic, but the words had an effect anyway. When he leaned over and kissed me, I didn't pull away. It seemed perfectly right and natural at the moment. And for the first time in two weeks—or possibly a lot longer—I felt comfortable. Maybe even *nice*. There was just one thing nagging me.

"Hungry?" he asked.

"Are you a mind-reader now?"

"No, I just heard your stomach growl. How about Pizza Hut?"

Pizza sounded really good, but I didn't feel like moving. "Can't we have it delivered? I don't feel like going out."

Brad actually smiled. "This might be one of the better neighborhoods, Jessica. But it's still Hell. How about if I go pick it up and we can have it here? Mushrooms and pepperoni?"

He paused at the door. "By the way, what you were asking about before, if you could print out book pages? I've actually been working on something like that for you. We can try it out later."

When he left, I picked up the newspaper he'd brought back. My mother wasn't in the main headline, but she was on the front page: "Hunsucker Campaign Gains Momentum."

I scanned the article with only the mildest of interest, which was all it warranted anyway. It was just a report on the upcoming primary elections, where Mommie Dearest was supposed to pick up a bunch of simple-minded delegates. But when I turned the page, I saw something that drew my attention. It was an editorial, and the title read "Hunsucker's Utopian Village."

One can only stand back in awe at the rapid rise of Margaret Hunsucker in the esteem of the American people. In declaring her candidacy, she seemed to be a nonstarter, expressing extreme right-wing views that could only appeal to a minority of voters. Her calls for an immigration policy based on race, religion, ethnicity, and sexual orientation recall an earlier century, and her suggestions for a deportation policy based on the same criteria carry a frightening echo

of the fascist governments America has fought in the past. She talks about dramatic changes in the Constitution and governmental structure, shifting significant power from the legislative to the executive branch, eliminating life terms for Supreme Court members and allowing the sitting president to select all judges.

But it is her vision of the world as it could be under her administration that has captured the imagination and enthusiasm of the public. As a result of her proposed policies, she guarantees security and tranquillity, not only in the United States but all over the world. She promises a cessation of wars, not only between nations but also an end to the internal conflicts that tear nations apart. She assures us that there will be an end to poverty and disease, not only at home but worldwide, with a special emphasis on third-world countries. A global utopia—who would not be in favor of that? If this could be achieved through her policies, would it matter how unusual those policies are?

There are those who feel she has not yet adequately demonstrated how her platform will accomplish these goals. But there are more who are beginning to trust her words. And it is trust that translates into votes.

Believing that my eyes were suddenly diseased or at least playing monstrous tricks, I read the editorial again. Then I closed the newspaper to look once more at the front page. Yes, it was still the newspaper I'd thought it was, a well-respected, nationally recognized left-of-center publication. Which had suddenly begun printing utter nonsense.

I was still pondering this mystery when Brad returned with the pizza. I gave the editorial to Brad to read while we ate, but when he finished, he wasn't as puzzled as I'd been. "Makes sense to me," he said.

I momentarily forgot the new affection I was feeling for him. "Are you crazy?" I yelled. "First of all, her plans are *sick*. It's not even a question of liberal or conservative anymore, she's nuts. She wants to change the Constitution, for crying out loud. And this is a real newspaper, not the *National Enquirer*! I know this newspaper, *you* know it, it's famous, it's like the most important newspaper in the world. How could it support her insane platform?"

Brad reached over for another slice. "The paper never said it was supporting her, it was just commenting on her."

"Without one word of real criticism," I pointed out. "And this is an editorial."

Brad shrugged. "You're forgetting something, Jess. Your mother made a pact with the devil. Who do you think is stronger? Satan or the *New York Times*?"

"But she's talking gibberish!" I wailed. "It's not even logical. What does a new Supreme Court have to do with ending poverty and disease in the third world?"

"She's a politician," Brad reminded me. "She says what she has to say to get elected. Who knows what she's really planning?"

For some reason, *I* wanted to know. "Can we look for her on TV tonight?"

Brad wasn't gung-ho. "I was kind of hoping we could get inside a movie theater. Maybe find a comedy, or . . . or a romance. Nothing pornographic," he added quickly. "Just something . . . happy."

"We could do that later," I promised. "Please? I'm just really dying of curiosity now. I want to know what she's up to."

"Yeah, yeah, okay," Brad relented. "I'll see what I can do."

With his computer-geek wisdom, Brad managed to figure out coordinates that would put us in Margaret Hunsucker's private office back at the house in the woods. She wasn't there, though. Only one person was in the room, a man I didn't recognize, who was sitting at her desk and typing on a desktop computer.

"Can we see what he's typing?" I asked Brad.

Brad fiddled with the remote, and shook his head. "No, I can't get the perspective."

A woman I recognized very well came into the office. Lisa looked nervous. "Are you finished with the memo?" she asked the man.

"Almost."

"Are you sure the firewall is up?"

"Absolutely," the man assured her. "There's no way anyone can hack into this."

"Hah," Brad muttered. "That's what they all think."

"Even so," Lisa said, "the second you've finished, we print out five copies. Then you delete the file and burn the notes."

"Got it," he said. "We're ready. Turn on the printer."

Brad picked up another control. "Perfect—we can test my copy-and-print program."

The printer in the office was positioned where we could see the pages coming out. They were too far away to read, but Brad used his gadget to photograph each sheet as it emerged, and before Lisa could snatch it out of the tray and out of view.

"The file's deleted," the man said. He tore two pages off the yellow legal pad on the desk, crumpled them, and tossed them into the metal wastebasket. From the TV came a whirring sound, and then a paper slid out onto the tray contraption Brad had attached to the back of it. Brad took it, but kept his eyes on the screen.

"You need to destroy the whole pad," Lisa ordered the man. "The impression from her pen might be readable."

"And you might be paranoid," the man muttered. "Okay, okay." He threw the pad into the basket, too. "You got a light?"

"No."

The man groaned. "Neither do I. That's the consequence of no-smoking laws. Nobody carries matches anymore."

Lisa fished the papers out of the wastebasket. "I suppose we could eat them."

"Wow!" Brad exclaimed.

"Yeah, Lisa's pretty hyper," I agreed.

"No, I'm talking about this memo."

I turned to see Brad reading the paper that had come out of our TV. His mouth was still open.

"What does it say? Don't tell me, let me guess. She's going to outlaw same-sex marriages. No, wait. . . . She's going to outlaw sex."

Brad whistled. "I hate to admit it, but, as a demon, I'm impressed. I gotta give this woman props for wickedness." He passed it to me, and I started to read.

It wasn't long before my head was spinning. If the editorial in the *New York Times* had been a slap in the face, this memo was more like a bullet to the brain.

Eleven

THE MEMO was breathtaking in its simplicity. It was a straightforward outline, a succinct, clear, and uncomplicated blueprint that presented the step-by-step process through which Margaret Hunsucker's version of the United States of America would take over the world.

For each nation, a study would be initiated to identify issues that were not held in consensus among the country's population. Some of the problems had been going on for ages—Christians fighting Muslims in Eastern European nations, Protestants against Catholics in Ireland, Arabs versus Jews in the Middle East—and Hunsucker's administration would just have to stoke the fires and keep them burning. Other potentially divisive elements within populations could be exploited—the rich against the poor, the light-skinned against the dark-skinned. Attention was drawn to social conventions that could get people worked up—fox hunting in England, bullfighting in Spain, legal prostitution in Holland, smoking everywhere, that sort of thing. There was no small issue that couldn't be built up and made more controversial.

A special covert U.S. organization would be in charge of recruiting citizens in each country to create disruptions based on these issues. Operatives would be trained in organizational skills, management, communications, and weaponry, and they would be given very specific instructions—where to hold demonstrations, which buildings to burn, who to attack and/or take hostage.

In the guise of providing assistance to the recognized government of the country, a CIA-type agency would then infiltrate the fray. Through careful use and prudent manipulation of the media, this agency would generate an increase in unrest and attacks, until the current government could be labeled as "terrorist" and overthrown. Established as a temporary and friendly occupation force, the United States could then go about the strategic elimination of opposing forces and economically useless populations. And as the nation recovered and found itself in a peaceful and prosperous condition, a puppet government would be set up under American control.

There was a note stating that variables based on the size of a country, its position and borders, the population figures, and its current political situation would be taken into consideration, but essentially the approach would remain the same for each nation or region.

And I saw how my mother would achieve this utopian world she was promising voters. If you control the world, you'll have security—it's not like you'd attack yourself, right? If everyone is on the same side, there will be no unrest, and— presto—tranquillity. You could even call it democracy. Run national elections, support the idea of majority rule—no problem, if you know in advance that everyone will vote for the same person. And if anyone couldn't be persuaded or coerced to follow the Hunsucker ideals, that person could just . . . disappear.

"This is unbelievable," I whispered. "No, it's worse than unbelievable. It's, it's—"

"Believable," Brad said. "What's more, it could actually work."

I gasped. "Brad!"

"Hey, I'm not saying I approve of it. I'm just saying that if you look at the logic behind the plan, it makes sense. If nobody disagrees about anything, there won't be any wars. Eliminate hunger, poverty, and disease? Easy as pie. Just eliminate the hungry, the poor, and the sick."

"But—but people, good people, they won't go along with this," I objected.

"Are you kidding? You read the editorial. They're already starting to buy into it. She's getting more and more popular."

Once again, I was in a position of trying to absorb the unthinkable. "So this is Satan's plan for the world."

"Whoa, hold on there!" Brad exclaimed. "Not that I want to defend him, but you can't put all the blame on Satan. There's still free will, you know, even when you cut a deal with the devil. This is your mother's idea. He just paved the way, gave her a little assistance. He likes to show his support for genuine and original depravity." He scratched his head. "Although I'm not so sure this is completely original. I've heard stories about Iraq, and Vietnam—"

"I don't care if it's original," I retorted. "It's horrendous. She has to be stopped."

"By who?" Brad asked.

"Oh, *please*, this is America we're talking about, not some sort of fascist totalitarian dictatorship."

"Not yet," Brad murmured.

I ignored that. "I'll bet there are demonstrations going on all over the place already. There have to be some kind of organized groups sprouting up. Can we search?"

With a sorrowful face, Brad picked up the remote. "Guess I can forget about seeing a movie tonight."

It wasn't easy, hunting down some real opposition. We started off with the satanic candidate herself, and lucked out—we found her at a rally. I made Brad hit the "mute" button—I couldn't bear hearing her syrupy voice mouthing her nauseating garbage—and searched the crowds for some indication of anti-Hunsucker activity. But there were no signs or banners, not even any people who looked unhappy.

Then we looked for the other candidates running for a party nomination. We found some giving speeches, or interviews. They talked about the usual stuff—domestic problems, the economy, foreign affairs—but no one mentioned Margaret Hunsucker. Which made sense, I supposed—they were all too busy promoting themselves to worry about the competition.

Next we hit university campuses, the ones that had reputations for activism. We came across a protest against a proposed tuition hike, a march calling for an environmentally friendly heating system for the classrooms, a demonstration demanding higher salaries for faculty. And a near riot that had something to do with broken snack machines in the residence halls. Nothing political at all.

"Damn," I muttered in frustration. "Doesn't anyone care? A maniac bitch is trying to take over the world, and they're worried about global warming."

Brad gave me a reproving look. "Global warming is a serious issue, Jessica. And believe me, Satan's got a hand in that, too."

"Okay, you're right. But world domination is more important than vending machines. Why isn't anyone taking action?"

As usual, Brad was reasonable. "Probably because they don't think there's anything going on that's worth taking action against. You read the editorial, Jess. No one knows the methods she plans to use to achieve her wonderful goals."

I indicated the paper I was still holding. "*We* know. And we've got the proof right here. Something has to be done, Brad. We have to tell people the truth about Margaret Hunsucker."

Now Brad looked pained. "Jessica—"

I didn't let him speak—I was on a roll now. "I've got an idea! The next time you go to earth for your job, you take this memo. You make a ton of copies, and you distribute them all over the place. Send them to newspapers, stick them on walls—"

Brad broke in. "*Jessica.*"

"What?"

"Nothing can be taken from this world to earth."

"Oh, come on, you smuggle things here all the time."

"Bringing stuff in isn't that hard. It's different when you're going out. Everyone's scanned for contraband."

I didn't get it. "How come the rules are so different for coming and going?"

Brad smiled. "Because everyone down here knows for sure that earth exists. But no one on earth can prove the existence of Hell. They want to keep it that way."

"By 'they' you mean Satan?"

"Yeah, supposedly he likes to keep people on earth guessing about what happens, you know, *after*. It gives the religions something to bond over." He raised his eyes. "Actually, I've heard they have a similar rule up there."

I considered this. "Maybe you could *talk* to people. . . ."

He was shaking his head before I could finish the sentence. "The only people who can see me are the people I'm there for."

I dropped the memo on the coffee table. "So she just goes on her merry way and makes her promises and nobody questions her?"

Brad raised his hands in a gesture of hopelessness. "I don't know what to tell you, Jess."

It would be impossible to explain what I was feeling right that moment. It went beyond frustration, way beyond. I could see the horror my mother would inflict on the world. I could sense the tyranny, the fear, the destruction. The lives lost, the people who remained becoming mindless robots. At least I knew that in the afterlife one still had a heart, because mine was pounding very hard and fast. And maybe breaking.

I looked at Brad. There was no mistaking the compassion in his eyes. Was he just feeling pity for me, or for all those lost souls up there? And what did it matter, if nothing could be done?

"Then she can do whatever she wants," I said. "And she's even got Satan on her side."

"If it's any consolation, he can't offer much help," Brad told me. "He's got a zillion deals like hers going on. She won't get any special guidance, and he won't be looking over her shoulder."

"I guess it doesn't matter," I said dully. "She's evil enough to get it done all on her own."

We sat in silence. Then Brad yawned, and stood up. "I'm going to bed."

I didn't say anything.

"Wanna come?" he asked, but there wasn't much hope in his voice.

Just a couple of hours earlier, I'd been thinking that this could be the night. But the mood had disappeared, and I shook my head.

"I'm just going to sit here and think a while." I could have gotten up and kissed him at least, but I didn't feel like moving.

He seemed to understand. "Well . . . good night."

"G'night."

After he'd left the room, I picked up the remote. I didn't really want to start searching again. I set the remote to "mute," so I wouldn't disturb Brad, and just aimlessly clicked on the preset channels.

The library was closed, and dark. Maybe tomorrow Brad would show me how to copy pages. I clicked and I was in my mother's dark, empty office. I went into a movie theater, but it was something in Swedish, and I wasn't in the mood to read subtitles.

The next place on the preset selection was Woodbridge. It was dark there, too, but I made out a couple of figures by the bulletin board, right next to the steps where I'd been picked up by the chauffeur a lifetime ago. Something about them looked familiar.

I hit the close-up button and caught my breath. Those same two guys were there, Sanders and Baggy Pants. And they were unscrewing the nails that were holding the glass to the board again. Had I turned on the reality history channel by mistake?

No, the poster they were putting on the board had nothing to do with poor Alton Crenshaw. In large print, the top line read: "Stop Hunsucker In Time."

The first letter of each word was bright red, and I noticed that they formed an acronym. Cute.

I thought about turning up the sound, but I didn't want to wake Brad. I studied the silent figures in fascination. So Sanders and his friend were anti-Hunsucker. A rush of tingly sensations filled me. I couldn't be sure if the feelings were

because someone shared my concern, or because that someone happened to be an amazingly good-looking guy I'd had
the hots for just a couple of weeks ago.

I heard Brad's bedroom door open, and for some (guilty?)
reason, I hit the "off" button. Glancing up, I saw him, wearing
those silly cocktail pajamas, standing in the entranceway to
the living room looking at me anxiously. Then he spoke.

"*You* could go."

TWELVE

I STARED at him stupidly as he sat down in the armchair. "I could go? To earth?"

He nodded.

"You mean, like, as a ghost or something?"

"No. Like a regular person."

"But how is that possible? I'm dead."

Brad rubbed his head. "Actually, I've been meaning to talk to you about that."

"About what? Being dead?"

"Yeah. You see . . . remember what I said about good and bad, how it's all relative?"

"Yes."

"Well, it's sort of the same thing with life and death."

I stared at him. "Brad, that doesn't make sense. A person is alive or dead, that's it. I mean, I know there are the medical definitions, like when people are brain-dead but they can be kept alive with machines. And all that stuff about near-death experiences, and going toward the light, but . . ." I stopped. Brad was shaking his head.

"I'm not talking about that kind of thing."

I was getting impatient. "Then what *are* you talking about?"

"It's kind of hard to explain." He grinned sheepishly. "Maybe that's just because I really don't understand it myself. It's like, no one's ever completely dead, like not existing. They just go into different forms."

"You mean reincarnation?"

He scratched his head again. "I'm not sure. I just know that everyone goes on *being*, up there or down here, and some people—depending on how they got here or there—well, they can go back."

I was stunned. "Permanently?"

He made another helpless gesture. "I don't know. There's a story, I don't know if it's true, about how Satan had this babe he really liked, but her mother had some sort of power over nature, and she was so upset about the daughter coming here that she made a lot of trouble on earth."

"Wait a minute," I said. "I know that story. It's a Greek myth."

"Whatever. Anyway, supposedly Satan made a deal with the mother, so the girl could spend part of the year on earth with her. And I've heard other stories, about people going back because they didn't finish doing something. Of course, it's usually something really evil and disgusting, but I don't know if that's a requirement."

I could feel the shiver of excitement traveling up my spine and the smile spreading across my face. "And you really think I could do that? Go back to earth?"

Brad didn't smile. "I can't make any guarantees. I'm just saying it's possible."

I couldn't remember ever seeing him look so serious. "Brad, is this dangerous? For you, I mean."

"I don't know. I guess it depends on . . . actually, I have no idea what it depends on. But you don't have to go yakking about it with Angie."

"I won't, I promise. I just don't want you getting into any trouble for this."

"Neither do I," Brad assured me fervently.

I looked at him curiously. "Why are you doing this? If it could turn into a big problem for you . . ." A thought struck me. "Brad, are you trying to get rid of me?"

"No!" And for the first time in this conversation, he made direct eye contact with me. "Jessica, you're the best thing that's ever happened to me."

"You mean, since you've been down here."

"No, I mean *ever*. But . . . but I can see how much this means to you. You'll never be happy here if you're always thinking about your mother screwing everything up on earth. Wait, 'happy' isn't the right word—nobody's *happy*, you're not supposed to be happy here. But you could be, I don't know, *comfortable*." He was watching me carefully now, as if looking for confirmation.

Only I couldn't give it to him. Because I didn't know if this was true.

He looked away. "Anyway, after what she did to you, you should have a chance to get even."

I had to smile. "Come on, Brad. You're not talking about my personal revenge. You know what I think?"

"What?"

"You don't want my mother to take over the world, either. Because it would be a very bad thing."

He was still looking past me. "Jessica, I'm a demon. I *support* bad things."

I moved over to his chair and sat on the arm of it. Then I took his face in my hands and turned it toward me. "Remember what you just told me, about nobody being completely dead? If that's true, then you can't completely stop being human, either." I leaned in closer and whispered in his ear: "Let's go to bed."

To my surprise, he shook his head. "No, not like this. Not because you're grateful." He kissed me, though, very sweetly. Then he stood up. "We'll work out the travel plans in the morning. Good night."

"Good night," I echoed. And I watched in wonderment as he went back down the hall to his bedroom.

Did I sleep well that night? I wasn't sure. The dreams I had were so natural and vivid that I woke up feeling like I'd been on the move all night. I couldn't remember exactly what happened in the dreams; all I knew was that I'd felt so alive, so energized, more real than I usually felt when I was awake.

I woke to a familiar smell. Brad was making French toast again. Quickly I washed up, dressed, and joined him in the kitchen.

"I thought I'd make this our Sunday tradition," he said, flipping over a slice in the frying pan.

Was it really Sunday again? My third Sunday in Hell? No, that couldn't be right. I'd left Woodbridge on a Saturday, Brad had come for me Saturday night. . . .

"What's the matter?" he asked.

"Nothing," I said. "I'm just confused. We arrived on a Sunday, and we went to McDonald's. You made the first French toast on a Monday."

"Oh. Well, you might be right. You lose track of the days here."

That was true. Without a class schedule and my regular TV shows, days of the week had come to mean nothing to me. "I wonder if I'll have a hard time getting used to life on earth again," I said.

Brad smiled. "You've only been away a couple of weeks,

Jess. I'm sure you'll adapt pretty quickly." He flipped the slices onto plates and brought them to the table. "Go ahead and use all the maple syrup you want—I've got a gig in Vermont tomorrow."

"Are you going to take me with you?" I asked him. "Is that how I'll get back to earth?"

He shook his head. "No, you're my partner, we'll definitely get noticed if we take off together. I just talked to a buddy of mine, and I can get you on a transport today."

"Today?" My heart quickened. I had no idea this could be organized so quickly.

"Yeah, and we have a lot to go over before you leave." Brad sounded very businesslike, as if he were sending me off to a convention. "First off, we have to decide where you're going."

"I have a choice?"

"Sure, you can go anywhere on earth." I opened my mouth, and he held up his hand to ward off my words. "And, *please*, don't ask me how it works. It's all molecular rearrangement, something to do with cells. Biology was never my thing. It works, that's all I know."

Since my only familiarity with travel to and from earth came from watching old *Star Trek* episodes, I couldn't resist asking, "Can I say 'Beam me up, Scotty'?"

Brad groaned. "You won't be the first. Now, listen carefully, I've got a lot of instructions."

"Maybe I should write them down."

"No, you have to memorize them, because you can't take anything with you from Hell, not even a piece of paper. So you need to go someplace where people won't ask a lot of questions. Maybe a homeless shelter. . . ."

"What about a school?"

He looked up. "What school?"

I began spreading the maple syrup so there would be

equal distribution across the slices of French toast. This demanded all my attention as I replied. Okay, it didn't really require all my attention, but I just didn't want to look Brad in the eye.

"After you went to bed, I took a look at my old boarding school, Woodbridge. And I saw a poster that was anti-Hunsucker. So I'm guessing there must be some kind of organized group there."

"A high-school organization?" Brad pondered doubtfully. "That can't be too powerful."

"It's a start," I said quickly. "Maybe through them I can get names, Web sites, find out what's really going on."

"Won't you be recognized?"

I shook my head firmly. "After I got this makeover, I couldn't even recognize myself. That's why my mother gave me the makeover for my birthday, remember? So if I got away from you no one would believe I was me. I'm not worried about that. But I'll have to come up with a new name, of course, and some sort of story that explains what I'm doing hanging around Woodbridge."

"And another story to explain why you know so much about Margaret Hunsucker."

I nodded. "Maybe I'll say I know someone who knows someone who knows someone. . . ." I made a face. I didn't sound very convincing.

"You have to be really discreet," Brad warned me. "Don't tell anyone who you really are. No one would believe you anyway, and you could end up in a nuthouse, or jail. Can you think of someone you know there who might be nice to a stranger? Give you a place to stay?"

Immediately I thought about Sanders. And just as immediately I hit the maple syrup again.

"Watch out, you're making a mess," Brad said.

"Sorry. Yeah, I'm sure I can come up with someone."

Brad was watching me, and his brow wrinkled up. "Your school, Woodbridge—it's an all-girls school, right?"

"Right." I still couldn't meet his eyes, and I switched to another topic. "Is there any way I can reach you while I'm there? In case of emergency?"

"You won't need to. I can watch you on TV, and I'll be able to see if you've got a problem. I won't spy on you," he added. "We can come up with a signal. When you want privacy, just tug on your right earlobe with your right hand. If I see that, I'll turn off the TV. Whatever you're doing, talking to people, getting ready to take a bath, it doesn't matter. You don't even need an excuse—maybe you just want to feel like you're really alone. Try it. Tug on your earlobe."

I tugged my earlobe with my thumb and forefinger. Brad gave me a thumbs-up. "It looks completely natural. Nobody will notice."

We spent the afternoon working on my cover stories, debating the credibility of one over another, making up background details, and, finally, choosing a name. With a common name like Jessica (there were three in one of my classes), I was all for giving myself something literary and memorable, like Cassandra or Desdemona, but Brad disagreed.

"You don't want to stand out, you want to blend in. What are some of the most popular names for girls now?"

"I don't want to be an Ashley or a Britney," I stated firmly.

We settled on something less popular, but common and easy for me to remember—Jane. "What about a last name?" I wondered. "Do I need one?"

"Most people use both their names when they introduce themselves," Brad remarked. "How about . . . Cameron?"

I tried it out. "Jane Cameron. It sounds like a normal name. How did you come up with Cameron?"

He gave me that cute lopsided smile. "That was my last name."

I tried *that* out. "Brad Cameron."

"Actually, it was Bradley. Bradley George Cameron."

"Bradley George Cameron," I repeated. "It sounds so—so respectable."

He shrugged. "'What's in a name? A rose by any other name would smell as sweet.' Shakespeare."

"Hey," I cried in delight, "you *have* read something!"

"*Julius Caesar,* right?"

"Close. *Romeo and Juliet.*"

He grinned. "We had to read both my junior year in high school, and I didn't read either of them."

"You know, you might want to give reading another chance," I told him. "Especially if we can start copying books from the television."

"Maybe you could help me pick out books you think I'd like."

Then it was time for me to go. At least I didn't have to do any packing. I put on the clothes I'd bought on earth—they really were great-looking, and nobody on earth had seen them except Lisa and the guy at the motel. I was good to go.

Brad drove me to the station, or whatever it was called. "There shouldn't be any problem," he said. "My pal Arnie's working today, and I've got the coordinates for him." He hesitated. "I'll probably watch you for a while today. Just to make sure you arrive safely. Is that okay?"

"Of course," I said quickly. "In fact, I'll feel better, knowing you've got your eye on me." I looked at him and smiled, but his eyes were on the road.

"Don't forget about the signal for privacy," he said.

"I won't." After a moment, I asked, "When will I come back? And how will I get here?"

He kept looking straight ahead. "We'll play it by ear. See how it goes. Then, when the time's right, I'll come pick you up."

We were there. It was a long, low building, with no identifying signs, and not many people around. "There's work being done on the building," Brad told me. "It's still operational, but most of the arrivals and departures have been shifted to a temporary station." He pulled up to a door, but he didn't turn the motor off. "Arnie's coming out to get you."

"Okay."

We sat in silence for a moment, and then a guy about Brad's age came out. Brad rolled his window down and motioned him over. "Arnie, Jessica. Jessica, Arnie."

"Hi," I said, and the guy nodded. He and Brad had a quick whispered discussion. Then Brad turned to me. "Go with Arnie."

I wasn't sure how to say good-bye. Arnie was standing right there, and Brad looked a little nervous, like he didn't want to hang out here long. I leaned over and kissed his cheek. "See ya."

"Have a safe trip," he murmured. We could have been any couple in the world, at any airport or train station, parting for a brief period. Or maybe not so brief.

I got out of the car and followed Arnie into the building. Walking down the corridor, we passed a couple of men in hard hats, but neither of them glanced at us. Arnie ushered me through a door into a narrow compartment that looked like one of those little satellite trains, the kind that take you from some airports to the actual plane. There were about a dozen seats, but I was the only passenger.

I sat down, and Arnie left. What now? I wondered.

That was the last thing I remembered thinking.

chapter
Thirteen

I WISH I could provide a more detailed description of the voyage. I wouldn't want this to sound like one of those children's books where someone goes through a closet or falls down a rabbit hole and ends up in a magical kingdom. Maybe there was something in the atmosphere of the train that drugged me, or the cabin pressure knocked me out—I don't know. Or maybe Scotty beamed me up.

All I know is, when I opened my eyes, I found myself sitting on the Mildred C. Spencer Class of 1931 Memorial Bench, just outside the gymnasium on the grounds of the Woodbridge School for Girls. I sat very still and took some time to absorb it all.

It was still Sunday. I knew that because there was an old church with bells down the road that rang out the hour on Sundays, and I heard them now. I counted them and checked my watch. Yes, it was six o'clock.

It was all so familiar that for one brief moment I thought maybe the last two weeks had been a dream, and that I'd never left Woodbridge at all. Carefully, on wobbly feet, I stood up, and walked over to the door of the building, where a window would give me some reflection of myself.

No, this wasn't the old Jessica Hunsucker with glasses and braces and long stringy hair who looked back at me. This was post-makeover Jessica Hunsucker. I corrected myself. This was Jane Cameron. Childhood friend of Jessica Hunsucker. Who had traveled across the country to come to her old friend's funeral.

I was mentally going over the details of my story when a girl in jeans and a sweatshirt came out of the building. She looked at me with a slightly puzzled expression, and I have no idea what she saw in *my* face. Not recognition, I hoped. It was Kip Simmonds.

"Um, can I help you?" she asked.

With all my practice and preparation, I was able to respond brilliantly. "Huh?"

"You don't go to school here, do you?"

Woodbridge had about two hundred students, but Kip was the type who'd be able to identify all of them. "No. I'm visiting."

As a fairly ritzy boarding school, Woodbridge was pretty security-conscious, and Kip was eyeing me with just a hint of distrust. "Who?"

I tried to rearrange my features so my expression would be in keeping with my story. "It's kind of hard to explain. Do you know—*did* you know Jessica Hunsucker?"

Kip's face hardened. "You're not from a newspaper, are you?"

"Oh, no," I assured her, though inwardly I was flattered to think that I looked sophisticated enough to be mistaken for an adult reporter. "Jessica was my best friend when we were little kids. I wanted to come to her funeral."

"You missed it," Kip told me. "And it wasn't here, anyway. It was somewhere around Leesburg."

"I know," I said. I took a deep breath and began to recite

from memory. "I'm Janie Cameron, I'm from the West Coast. I was driving here, but my car broke down, somewhere in Oklahoma. So I took a train, but I had to change so many times that by the time I got to Virginia it was too late. I went to the cemetery to pay my respects, and would you believe it, I was mugged! At the cemetery! This creep took my suitcase, my wallet, *everything*. I didn't know what to do. And then I remembered Jessica went to school here. So I hitchhiked from Leesburg, and I thought maybe I could find a friend of Jessica's to stay with until I can get some money from home." I didn't realize I'd told this whole story on one breath until I finished and started coughing.

Kip still seemed a little dubious. "Why didn't you go to the police?"

I was prepared for this question, and as soon as I could control the cough, I answered. "Oh, my parents would *kill* me! It could get into the papers, and they're very private people."

This was the kind of attitude any notable or even just social-climbing Woodbridge girl would understand. Kip relaxed and nodded. "I know what you mean."

"I just need to make some phone calls, and find a friend who can wire me some money. And . . . and maybe a place to stay tonight, because I won't be able to get money till tomorrow."

"You can use my phone," Kip said. "And I can check to see if there's a free bed in the dorm."

"Oh, thank you, so much!" I gushed. "You are *so* going to be invited to stay with me in Malibu!"

I hoped Brad was watching. I don't think he really believed that nobody would recognize me at Woodbridge. But as we walked to the residence hall, I passed girls who had been in my classes, girls I'd seen every day when I was a student here. Kip spoke to some of them—she even introduced me. Not one of them knew me. Kip had evidently bought the story Brad and I had concocted together, and I'd told it well. He might scold me for calling myself Janie instead of Jane, but I just thought Janie sounded friendlier.

Then there I was, back in my old residence hall. There was no great rush of emotion—I hadn't stayed there very long, so I didn't have any sentimental feelings for the place. Still, it was a little strange, being back on the hall where I used to live. Kip's room was just a few doors down from my old room.

Kip pointed to the desk. "There's the phone. I'll give you some privacy."

That was a bonus I hadn't expected. I'd been worried about faking a phone conversation, afraid she might be able to tell that I wasn't connected to anyone. But Kip closed the door and left me alone in the room.

I spoke softly, in case she was standing right outside the door. I didn't need a phone.

"Brad? I hope you're watching. I think I handled that pretty well! I'm sure she'll find me a bed for tonight, and first thing tomorrow I'll start tracking down the anti-Hunsucker group. Hopefully, I'll make contact and someone will put me up. But I just had an idea how I could maybe get my hands on some money, so I might be able to get my own hotel room and not have to bunk down with anyone." I grinned. "Watch me."

I opened the door. Kip wasn't there, so the first possible obstacle was overcome. There were two more to go. Would I be able to get into my old room? And had it been cleaned out yet?

I turned the handle on the door. It moved. And when I opened the door, I had to restrain myself from crying out for joy. The room was just as I'd left it. There was even the granola bar I'd meant to take with me on the trip to Leesburg but had forgotten and left behind on my bureau. I tore it open and took a huge bite. I was hungry, and who knew when my next meal would be.

Then I opened the top drawer and rummaged around. I found some change—a couple of quarters, and smaller coins. That wouldn't get me very far. If only I'd left a credit card, a bank ATM card, something like that. . . .

A memory made me catch my breath. Taking the credit card off the desk of the stoner at the motel.

I stuck my hand in my jeans pocket, and wanted to cry with relief when I felt the plastic edge of the card. How had it managed to come through with me? Brad had said there was work going on—maybe things weren't completely in order. And who cared anyway? I took the credit card out of my pocket and examined it in delight. There was another year before it would expire.

There was still a possible obstacle. The card could have been canceled after my so-called death. But there was also the very real possibility that no one would have thought about it. The card could be in perfectly good working order. Of course, I wouldn't be able to use it for long. Once someone on my mother's staff saw the account, it would be assumed the card had been stolen, and it would be canceled. And I couldn't buy anything—someone would recognize the name on the card. But I'd still have a day or two, maybe even a week, to get some cash with it. . . .

"What are you doing?"

I hadn't even heard the door open. I moved quickly to get the card back into my jeans pocket. "I wanted to see Jessica's room."

"And steal her stuff," Kip finished. "What did you just put in your pocket?"

Janie Cameron wasn't any more capable of looking sweet and innocent than Jessica Hunsucker would be. "Uh, nothing."

Kip glared at me sternly. "I'm going to call Security."

She would, too. Kip was that kind of girl. Reluctantly, I pulled the card out of my pocket. "I thought I'd bring this to her mother," I said. "You know, a keepsake."

"Sure." Kip stood aside, clearing the doorway but keeping the door open. "Give me the card. And get out."

I could envision Brad sitting on the turquoise sofa, and I could see his face as he watched this on TV. Sighing, rolling his eyes, shaking his head. With my head down—mainly for *his* benefit, not Kip's—I left the room, walked down the hall, through the lobby, and out the door.

In front of the building, I hesitated, trying to think of what I could do next. The bulletin board where Sanders had put up the poster was just by the steps. When Kip and I arrived, we'd come from the other side of the building, so I hadn't had a chance to look at it then. I did so now.

STOP
HUNSUCKER
IN
TIME

What I hadn't noticed when I saw the sign on the TV screen were the smaller words underneath. There was a meeting, and it was tonight. At seven-thirty, in the Dobbs Hall Common Room at St. Andrews. I smiled. "Wow. Did I luck out or what?"

Two passing students looked at me curiously, since I appeared to be talking to myself. For a fleeting moment, I actually considered telling them I was speaking to a demon in Hell. I didn't. It might have given Brad a chuckle, but I might have been carted off to a mental ward.

I walked down the circular driveway and headed in the

direction of St. Andrews. I'd never spent any time on the campus, but I'd passed it going to and from Woodbridge. It was about two miles up the road. Along the way, I kept up a stream of conversation with Brad.

"Maybe I'll find someone at the meeting who will put me up."

I imagined Brad responding: *Isn't St. Andrews an all-male school?*

"Yes, but it must be an open meeting if they posted it at Woodbridge. I'm sure there will be some girls there, too."

I can't believe how you screwed up back there.

"Yeah, that was stupid of me. If only I'd realized the card was in my pocket all along!" I felt like I was actually talking to him. It was funny how I could predict what he would say. I marveled at how well you can get to know someone when you've spent time alone with that person, even if just for two weeks.

It was just after seven when I arrived on the St. Andrews campus. This school was older than Woodbridge, and the buildings had a lot of ornate carving on them. One of them—the administration building, I think—had gargoyles on the cornices above the top windows. They were grotesque creatures, stone monsters, half human, half animal. I'd read something about gargoyles once. Supposedly, they were put on buildings back in the Middle Ages because people thought the demon images would scare off real demons. I tried to imagine a stone Brad up there on the ledge.

I smiled. Brad couldn't scare a fly. "Can you tell what I'm thinking right now?" I asked softly.

"What?"

I turned, and saw the skinny guy in baggy jeans who had been with Sanders the first time I saw him. "Sorry, just thinking out loud."

He started to walk on, but I said, "Wait!" He stopped and looked at me with apprehension.

"Can you tell me where Dobbs Hall is?"

He hesitated, as if he was unsure how to respond, and then he must have decided I didn't look like a complete lunatic. "That's where I'm going."

I took that as an unspoken invitation to come along with him. "Are you going to the anti-Hunsucker meeting?"

He grunted an assent. Then he added, "Shit."

"Excuse me?"

"That's what we call it. SHIT. Stop Hunsucker In Time."

"Right. I saw that on the poster at Woodbridge."

"You go to Woodbridge?"

"No, I was just, uh, visiting someone."

Fortunately, the guy didn't have a whole lot of curiosity, and he didn't ask any more questions. But *I* had questions.

"Are there a lot of people in the group?"

He shrugged. "I dunno. This is the first meeting."

"Why are *you* against Hunsucker?"

He shrugged again. "She's a bitch."

I couldn't argue with that. On the other hand, I wondered if he knew anything else about her.

The Common Room at Dobbs Hall was one of those formal rooms that try to look terribly English, and there wasn't anything common about it. There were chairs with velvet cushions, mainly green, and Oriental rugs on the floor. The walls were paneled in dark wood, and there were a lot of portraits of men in fancy gilded frames. Old Andrewsians, I figured, or whatever they called their alumni.

Four boys and one girl were there. The boys were in a group, sprawled on furniture or sitting on the floor, and none of them was Sanders. Baggy Pants joined them. The girl was on the other side of the room, standing by a table. She looked like she was a couple of years younger than me, too thin, with long, superstraight honey-blond hair. She wore skintight jeans, even tighter than mine, but with three-inch stiletto heels. I figured that was how they were supposed to be worn, not with sneakers, like I had on. And a little baby-doll-style pink top, not an ordinary T-shirt. I knew this had to be "the look" this season. She just seemed to be the kind of girl who would wear whatever was in, even if it made her look like a slut. Which it did.

She had a large round tin container in her hands, and she put it on the table. I strolled over there as she was opening it. There were cookies inside.

"Those look good," I said.

"I made them," the girl informed me. She stared at me for a minute, without smiling. I kept staring at the cookies. Finally, with clear reluctance, she said, "You can have one if you want."

I accepted the invitation. "Thanks."

Her eyes were still on me as I took a bite. I chewed, swallowed, and spoke. "These are delicious." I meant it, too—they were crunchy, with gooey chocolate chips.

She made a noise that might have been a "thank you," but I wasn't sure. I didn't want to say "you're welcome" in case she might think I was criticizing her for *not* saying thank you.

"I'm Janie Cameron."

She looked like she was being forced at gunpoint to respond. "My name is Ashley Easton." After a few seconds, she added, "I'm Bayne's sister."

"Who's Bayne?"

She raised her eyebrows. "You just walked in with him."

"Oh, him. I asked him for directions here. We didn't really

meet." The eyebrows went up again. Had I offended her? "But I'm happy to know his name," I added quickly. "He seems really nice."

"He has a girlfriend," Ashley warned me.

"Well, that's . . . that's good. Can I have another cookie?"

"If you really want one."

I did, and I took it. "Aren't you going to have any of your cookies?"

"Are you kidding?" she asked me. "Each one only has about a gazillion calories."

I looked back at the boys. More had joined the group, but none of them was Sanders. There weren't any other girls.

"Bayne's girlfriend can't come," Ashley said. "She goes to Woodbridge."

I then remembered Woodbridge's Sunday-evening curfew of eight o'clock. It had been instituted to make girls come back early from weekends away, so they'd be fresh for Monday classes. Hah—all parents had to do was send them back with a note or call the school and the students could arrive whenever they wanted.

"So you don't go to Woodbridge," I commented.

"*Obviously,* since I'm here. Where do you go to school?"

"Um, not around here. I'm just passing through."

Ashley didn't like that answer. Her eyes narrowed. Then she looked at her watch. "I wish Jordan would get here."

"Who's Jordan?" I asked. "Your boyfriend?"

She actually smiled, but it was a coy smile, like she was trying to be mysterious. "Maybe. Hopefully, very soon."

"Cool," I said without any interest at all. "Who's in charge of this meeting?"

"Jordan." She gave a tiny gasp. "Oh, here he comes."

I turned toward the door, and almost choked on my cookie. It was Sanders.

Nice name, Jordan Sanders. "Sanders Jordan" would have been okay, too. A lot of kids nowadays had names like that, where the first name could have been the last name and vice versa. Like my roommate at the school I went to before Woodbridge. When I saw her name on her suitcase label, it read "Shannon Blair." I called her Shannon several times before she pointed out the comma between the two names on the tag. And even after I knew, I was always slipping and calling her Shannon instead of Blair.

And why was I thinking about Blair Shannon at that moment? Because I was trying very hard to think about anything other than the fact that my initial reaction to him had been right on target. This guy was unbelievably hot.

Jordan Sanders, Jordan Sanders . . . no, I wouldn't forget the order of *his* names. He was just as I'd remembered him, better even. The shaggy blond hair, the blue eyes—he still had his tan, too. And that smile, it was magnetic. Maybe Ashley and I were the only ones who were massively turned on, but Jordan Sanders immediately grabbed the attention of everyone there. All the guys who'd been lounging around the room suddenly woke up, turned to him, and called out greetings. I couldn't take my eyes off him. And he was moving in my direction.

Well, not really. "Hey, babe," he said to Ashley. "Wow, you made those cookies I like!"

Ashley looked like she'd been lit up from inside. She practically shoved the tin at him. "Have some," she urged.

He took the tin but put it down on a nearby bookcase. "Later," he said. "I want to get this meeting started." He glanced in my direction. "Hi."

"Hi," I replied brightly. "I'm Janie Cameron, and I *really* hate Margaret Hunsucker."

I wasn't sure if he heard me. He'd hoisted himself onto

the table and sat there with his legs dangling, his hands gripping the edges. Very cool position, casual but confident and totally in control. When he spoke, he didn't need to raise his voice. The room had already gone completely silent, and everyone was looking at him.

"Hi, guys," he said easily. "Okay, we all know why we're here. We're worried. A lot of you are like me—we're going to turn eighteen before the next presidential election. That means we get to vote." He grinned. "You know, in some countries, they think it's very strange, here in the good ol' U.S. of A., that we can vote at eighteen but we can't drink legally till we're twenty-one. And a lot of you wish it was the other way around."

There were a couple of appreciative nods, and one guy whistled his approval. Jordan nodded in agreement. "Yeah, I can dig it. A couple of beers can make you happy, and there ain't much happening in the political arena that'll do that for you." There were more nods of agreement. "I mean, when was the last time anyone could say they felt happy about our government, the president, the way this country's being led?"

Suddenly his smile disappeared. "But there's a great big difference between having a president you disagree with, and having a president who could destroy the universe. That's what we're up against now. Have you been looking at the polls lately? Somehow, some way, a very dangerous person has become very popular among the American people. This is disturbing, folks. Or maybe I should say terrifying, and it wouldn't be an exaggeration. This woman is extremely scary.

"We gotta turn this thing around. Margaret Hunsucker has to be stopped. In time. Before she can wreak unbelievable, incomprehensible damage on our country. On our world."

The dozen or so people in the room burst into applause. I would have applauded, too, except I was too busy gaping.

How did he know? Had the memo I'd read become publicly available?

"The people have to be convinced that voting for this woman is not in the best interests of anyone. They have to learn the truth about her. They have to realize how bad she really is. Now, you're probably thinking, What's the point? What can a dozen high-school students do about a candidate for president? Well, there are more like us out there, and we have to unite. Tomorrow, there's going to be a massive anti-Hunsucker demonstration in D.C. And we're going to be there. It's all arranged. We've got a bus that'll take us there in the morning. There's a youth hostel that can put us up tomorrow night. Start packing."

A buzz went through the room, and a hand went up. "We got classes tomorrow," the boy said.

"Classes!"

I jumped. Not only had the volume of Jordan's voice increased, the whole laid-back, easygoing style had vanished.

"You're thinking about classes when we're on the eve of destruction, of total annihilation? Are you worried about getting demerits? Getting kicked off the soccer team? Losing weekend privileges? Believe me, those are not going to be your chief concerns if Margaret Hunsucker becomes president of the United States of America. You're going to be wondering where your personal liberties have gone—and whatever happened to the Constitution, and the Bill of Rights, and all those freedoms you take for granted. You'll have bigger things to worry about, like going off to a foreign land to fight and die in a war that has nothing to do with us. Well, guess what, folks? Saving the world may just be worth risking a few demerits."

This time, taking into account that there were still only a

dozen or so people in the audience, the applause was practically deafening. Guys stood up, raising their fists and yelling out their support. You could see how carried away they were.

I was carried away, too; there was no doubt about that. And I wasn't even thinking about blond hair and white teeth and blue eyes. I wanted to save the world, too.

Jordan Sanders—five minutes ago, he'd been a cute, cool high-school senior with a great body and a lot of charm. Now he was . . . like a savior. I'd heard of charisma, but I'd never seen it before in action. Jordan Sanders could have been the poster boy for charisma; his photo could have replaced the dictionary definition. I'd always considered myself to be a pretty down-to-earth person, who wasn't easily swayed by words and dramatic gestures. But at that moment, I knew I'd follow Jordan Sanders anywhere.

I approached him, but it wasn't easy getting close. I'd have to wait for the crowd around him to break up.

"The meeting's over."

That came from Ashley, standing by my side and eyeing me warily. "I just want to ask Jordan about the trip tomorrow," I said.

"I don't think there's any more room on the bus," Ashley said quickly.

I smiled. I'd never seen a bus that would hold only twelve people. I waited till there was an opening in the circle and moved in.

"Jordan?"

He looked at me blankly.

"We just met," I said. "I'm Janie Cameron. I was wondering if I could come tomorrow."

"Absolutely," he said. "The more, the merrier."

I considered flashing a triumphant smile in the direction of Ashley but decided it would be childish.

Ashley shot back immediately: "Jordan, that was a tremendous speech. Listen, I'm going to make some signs for the demonstration tomorrow. Want to help me come up with some good slogans?"

He was about to walk away with her, and frantically I searched my mind for something to say that might keep his attention on me for another minute. It didn't take me long.

"I knew Jessica Hunsucker," I blurted out.

His eyes widened. "You did?"

I hadn't planned on continuing with this story after leaving Woodbridge, but why not? Having contact with Jessica could explain why I had access to some of Margaret Hunsucker's plans.

"We were childhood friends," I told him. "I haven't seen her since we were in fourth grade, but we stayed in touch. I live on the West Coast now, but when I heard she died, I came out here for her funeral." I gave him the same story I'd given Kip, about the car and the robbery.

Jordan regarded me with interest. "I met her once," he said.

"Jessica?" I worked up a look of innocent surprise. "Really?"

"Yeah, it was the day before she was kidnapped. Over at Woodbridge, where she went to school."

"Jordan, you never told me that!" Ashley exclaimed. She made it sound like he told her everything, but she could have been faking it for my benefit.

I couldn't resist asking: "Was she nice? Did you like her?"

"She seemed okay. I remember being completely surprised when I found out who she was. It's hard to believe Margaret Hunsucker could have given birth to someone so normal."

I hadn't expected more, but, still, I was a little disappointed. "Normal" meant "ordinary." "So you thought she was just . . . okay."

"I didn't get to know her. We only had a two-minute conversation." He thought for a minute. "About Alton Crenshaw."

I faked surprise again. "The man who was just executed. That was a disgrace. And not just because he might have been mentally challenged. I'm completely opposed to capital punishment."

"Yeah, me, too."

"Of course," Ashley broke in. "No intelligent person could support capital punishment. I don't care what anyone says, it's cruel and unusual punishment." She raised her eyes and spoke solemnly. "I only hope he's in a better place now."

I didn't correct her.

"Do you really believe Jessica was killed by terrorists?" I asked.

Jordan shrugged. "I don't know. Who else? It wasn't for money. There weren't any ransom demands."

"Maybe . . ." I tried to choose my words carefully. "Maybe her mother arranged it. To get the public's sympathy."

He was clearly taken aback. "You think she'd have her own daughter killed?"

"Why not? She's a monster." Was I expressing a little too much feeling? "I mean, like you said. Evil. I wouldn't put it past her to do something like that."

He cocked his head to one side and looked at me thoughtfully. "Did you ever meet her?"

I shook my head. "But Jessica used to write me about her. You wouldn't believe the things she told me."

"I'd like to hear about it," he said.

We were interrupted by Baggy Pants—what was his name? Bayne. Another one of those upscale last-name first names. He broke in. "Sanders, I gotta go. C'mon, Ash."

Jordan turned to me. "Where are you staying, Janie? Do you need a lift?"

It was the first time he'd used my "name." I was inordinately pleased. "Actually"—I bit my lower lip—"I don't have a place to stay. I thought I could bunk down over at Woodbridge, but there weren't any free beds."

"You can't stay here," Jordan said. "They're really strict about girls in the dorm, and there's a counselor on every hall. Bayne and his sister live at home in town. Ashley, you got room at your house?"

Ashley stiffened. "I don't think so."

"You got two beds in your room, idiot," Bayne said. "You're not going to sleep in both of them."

Ashley set her lips in a tight line. "I'd better call Mom first."

"She won't care," Bayne said impatiently. "C'mon, let's go."

Jordan put an arm lightly around Ashley's shoulders. "Thanks, Ashley. That's the kind of thing we do in a movement like this, help each other out. We're all in it together."

I thought Ashley would melt right then and there. She put on a sickly-sweet smile that remained in place till we got into her brother's car. From the front passenger seat, she turned around to me.

"I don't know if the sheets on the other bed in my room are clean." I understood that to mean that if the sheets weren't clean I shouldn't expect them to be changed.

"That's okay," I said. "I can sleep anywhere."

Bayne made a snorting sound that I took for a laugh, and Ashley smirked knowingly. I was too tired to reword my comment. I sat back, closed my eyes, and hoped I wouldn't wake up in the middle of the night to find her covering my face with a pillow.

Actually, by the time I came out of the bathroom (after washing up with one of those tiny pink rosebud guest soaps, and rubbing toothpaste over my teeth with a finger), she was already asleep. With my own eyes already half closed, I got into the other bed, thinking I'd crash immediately, but something kept me awake. It was like there was some sort of unfinished business in my head, and I couldn't figure out what it was. I went over my mental to-do list. I'd made contact with the anti-my-mother group, I was set to go to a demonstration, my mission was in motion, I'd brushed my teeth—what was missing here?

I opened my eyes.

"Good night, Brad," I whispered.

Now I could sleep.

chapter
Fourteen

"IS THIS it?" I asked in dismay. In my mind, word of Jordan's plan had spread far and wide, and there would be a massive crowd of sign-bearing demonstrators waiting in front of the drugstore to take on Washington, D.C., and Margaret Hunsucker. There were only five, and that included me, Bayne, and Ashley.

Ashley regarded me in disdain. "The bus is stopping first at Woodbridge and St. Andrews."

I didn't know whether to feel relieved or alarmed. More people would be better for our cause—but what if the Woodbridge contingent included Kip Simmonds? I didn't want word of my so-called attempt at credit-card theft reaching the noble Jordan Sanders.

The bus came into view. Ashley immediately moved to the curb, and I knew why. She wanted to be first on the bus, so she could take the seat next to Jordan if it was free. Should I battle her for it? I wondered. She was a waif, and I was taller and bigger than she was. On the other hand, a girl with a crush the size of Ashley's could probably turn into Xena the Warrior Princess if she felt sufficiently threatened.

It turned out not to matter. When the bus stopped in front of us and the doors opened, Jordan hopped off. "Go ahead and get on the bus," he called out to our group. "I want to buy some gum."

As he went into the drugstore, the driver came out of the bus and began putting suitcases into the storage hold. I didn't have anything to give him, but I waited around anyway while Bayne and the other two got on the bus. Ashley glared at me, and I gave in. I really couldn't afford to make any major enemies here.

There were around fifteen people on the bus, so there were plenty of seats left. I took a window seat, looked around, and saw that Kip was not among the occupants. There were a couple of girls who could have come from Woodbridge, but I didn't know them. From the window, I could see Ashley still lingering behind, but then the driver closed the storage compartment and ordered her onto the bus. Looking very unhappy, she got on, came down the aisle, shot me one narrow-eyed glare, and sat down at the window seat just in front of mine. Like me, she had an empty aisle seat next to her.

Jordan strolled out of the drugstore, tossing his head so his hair moved off his forehead. Did he know how incredibly sexy that little motion was? He climbed onto the bus and started down the aisle. I could feel the suspense building inside me, and I flashed what I hoped was a dazzling smile. (In all honesty, I had to admit that I owed Lisa and my mother a debt of gratitude for getting those braces off my teeth.)

From where I sat, I couldn't see Ashley's face, but I suspected she, too, was presenting Jordan with her most seductive look. Maybe she was even licking her lips with the tip of her tongue, to add to the allure, because Jordan did wink at her as he approached. But he passed her row and sat in the seat next to mine.

I didn't flatter myself—with no makeup, and after a night of sleeping in my clothes, I couldn't be looking all that irresistible. I was sure he just wanted to find out what I could tell him about Margaret Hunsucker. Even so, it was a pleasure to find myself in such close proximity with someone who was so damned gorgeous.

"Hi," he said easily. "Glad you could make it. Everything okay?"

"Yes, fine, perfect," I prattled stupidly. I should respond with some kind of similar question, I knew that, but what? *How are you?* Too formal. Or maybe just *You?* "How about you? Everything okay?" Oh, boy, was that feeble, repeating what he'd just asked me.

"Great. You said you're from the West Coast, right? California?"

I nodded.

"Whereabouts?"

I figured I might as well continue with the story I'd given Kip. "Malibu."

He was interested. "There's a guy at St. Andrews from Malibu. You know Greg Wolfson?"

I swallowed. "No." But my mind was saying, Oh, no no no no no, and he's on this bus, and he's going to want to talk about Malibu, and all I know is what I've seen on TV. There's a beach.

"Too bad he couldn't make it today," Jordan said, and I almost fainted with relief. "I'm surprised you don't know him; he's the kind of guy who gets around. And Malibu's not that big, is it? What's the population?"

"I really don't know it all that well. My family just moved there. We move around a lot—my father's in the army—and I go to school in, in North Dakota, so I haven't spent much time in Malibu, so . . . so . . ." I was getting in way too deep. "So tell me about *you!*"

He was looking at me curiously, and all I could think of

was that quote about what a tangled web we weave when first we practice to deceive.

"Boston, born and bred," he said, "and that's about it."

"That's nice," I said. "Boston's a cool town. I mean, that's what I've heard. I've never actually been there."

He leaned across me to peer out the window. "Hope it's not going to rain."

I made another of my profound observations. "I guess that wouldn't be good for a demonstration."

"No kidding. And I'm really looking forward to this. To be able to do something, not just talk."

"Do you think there will be a lot of people at the demonstration?" I asked him.

"Who knows? I hope so. I'm guessing there may be a lot of closet Hunsucker-haters out there, but it takes guts for people to admit they're not crazy about her. The newspapers are already referring to the anti-Hunsucker groups as crackpots and nutcases."

"Unbelievable," I said. "Really unbelievable. Why are people buying into this crap? Everything she says, it's, it's like, you know, just unbelievable!" What I really couldn't believe was how inarticulate I'd suddenly become. I could visualize Brad watching this and laughing. What was it about Jordan Sanders that was reducing me to a blithering idiot?

But Jordan turned very serious and nodded slowly, as if I'd just come out with something terribly wise.

"She's pandering to the anxiety of the majority," he said. "They're scared. They're worried about terrorism, and the U.S. losing its position in the world, and that there's some great moral deterioration going on here that's ruining the nation. They're seeing parallels with the Roman Empire, and they're anticipating a decline and fall."

Wow, could he talk. And all I could do was bob my head up and down and say, "Yes, I know what you mean."

"Margaret Hunsucker is trying to harness the fears of the American people and channel them into support for her agenda. Her *secret* agenda. We don't even really know what it is."

I do, I said to myself, but I hadn't yet decided exactly how I would tell him what I knew. "How did you get interested in this?" I asked.

"I'm a sucker for a cause. When I see something that's just *wrong*, like an injustice, or discrimination, or someone trying to put something over on someone else . . . I have to *do* something. I can't just sit back and watch people be used and abused. The world can be a better place if people would just get involved." He gave me an abashed smile. "I know, I sound like an unrealistic idealist, don't I? Taking the moral high ground and all that."

"No," I said. "You sound like someone who cares."

"Some friends say I care too much. They're always on my case."

I was ready to take on those so-called friends. I thought he was wonderful.

"Have you heard about some of Hunsucker's ideas?" he asked. "She wants to make it legal for employers to take age and race and sexual orientation into consideration when they hire people! She says people shouldn't have to work with someone they don't feel comfortable with. And get this—she doesn't think the government should support day care, because women should stay home and take care of their kids. And she's actually upfront about it!"

I hadn't heard about this, but I wasn't surprised.

He went on. "But in my opinion, what's even more

frightening are these big promises she's making to people. She says she's going to eradicate poverty. How?"

I knew the answer to that one. "By getting rid of poor people."

"That sounds about right," Jordan said. "It's like Times Square in New York. My parents were just there, and they were raving about how it's changed, how there aren't any homeless people begging in the streets and sleeping in the doorways anymore. But where are those homeless people now? Not in homes. Some mayor just pushed them out of Times Square, and now they're in other boroughs, where tourists like my parents won't have to look at them. That mayor didn't eradicate homelessness any more than Hunsucker's going to eradicate poverty." He shook his head wearily. "I don't know where she's going to hide them all."

Again, I knew the answer. "She'll deport them. Or worse."

"She hasn't said much about her foreign policy, and I can't even imagine what that's going to be all about."

I told him. "She's going to use spies to generate unrest and revolutions in other countries. Then she'll send the U.S. in to take over."

"Hey, you've got quite an imagination," Jordan commented, smiling.

"No, I don't," I said. "It's true. This is what she's planning to do. I learned this from Jessica."

I could have sworn his tan was fading before my very eyes. "Are you serious?"

"Yep. And I meant what I said about getting rid of poor people, too. That's way up there on her agenda."

"Jessica Hunsucker told you this?"

"She wrote it. In an e-mail."

He was more than intrigued, I could see it in his eyes. "Do you still have the e-mail?"

I dropped my eyes. "No. I deleted it."

"Damn," he swore. "A little evidence would be great." He thought for a minute. "Do you know any computer geeks? Maybe someone could work on your hard drive and retrieve it."

I wondered if Brad was watching. I certainly had the computer-geek friend. Unfortunately, the computer didn't exist. It was time to change the subject.

"Um, could I have a stick of gum?"

He looked at me blankly. "What? Oh, no, sorry, I don't have any."

"I thought that's what you went into the drugstore for."

He lowered his voice. "That was my excuse to get off the bus. So Ashley couldn't sit with me. She's a sweet kid and all, and she's my best friend's sister, but I really wanted to talk to you."

I refused to let myself feel good about that. He wasn't attracted to me, he was only interested in the Hunsucker connection.

The bus pulled into a rest stop, and the driver told us we had five minutes. Everyone got out to stretch, and I joined the line at the bathroom. When I got back inside the bus, Ashley had taken my seat. She gave me a victorious look, Jordan gave me a helpless one. I just smiled and took Ashley's old seat.

Despite my annoyance, I actually approved of the fact he didn't tell Ashley to get out of my seat. He was a nice person, and he didn't want to hurt the girl's feelings. This was the kind of thing Brad would do, I thought. Although I couldn't really see someone like Ashley having a crush on Brad. Brad had wonderful qualities, of course. But Jordan . . . Jordan was something else.

I was still reeling from what I'd just learned about him. All that passion and idealism—he was so honorable! He had the characteristics of a revolutionary leader. I could see his face on posters and T-shirts, like Che Guevara. And at that moment, I was thankful that Brad could only see and hear me, he couldn't read my mind.

We arrived in the D.C. suburbs, and the bus took us to the youth hostel. Jordan joined me by the bus as the driver put the last of the suitcases on the sidewalk and closed the compartment. Ashley was by his side.

"Where's your bag?" he asked.

"I don't have one," I replied. "I told you I was mugged, remember? I lost everything. I don't even have a toothbrush."

Ashley raised her eyebrows. "You didn't brush your teeth this morning?" Her expression changed. "You didn't use *my* toothbrush, did you?"

Jordan peered down the street. "I'm sure you can buy a toothbrush around here somewhere."

"I don't have any money, either," I said simply. "No wallet, no ATM card."

Jordan looked at his watch. "Ashley, would you take my bag into the hostel? Thanks, babe." He grabbed my hand. "We've got a couple of hours before the demonstration. C'mon." He waved at a passing taxi and pulled me toward it, leaving behind a girl who I could safely presume was not terribly happy.

chapter
Fifteen

JORDAN TOLD the driver what we needed, and it only took five minutes for the man to drop us in the parking lot of a strip mall, which bore a distinct resemblance to the one Brad had pointed out last week. In fact, this whole area could have been an upscale version of Hell. The houses were a little bigger, and the lawns were better kept, but the neighborhood still looked extremely dull, and the short stretch of highway we took must have had eight fast-food restaurants in a row.

Jordan apparently had some bucks. He told the taxi driver to wait, and first we went into one of those gigantic we-have-everything-you-want pharmacies. He graciously waited for me by the magazine rack while I ran around picking up all the little personal items I needed, and then he paid for them all. I promised him I'd pay him back, but he kept saying not to worry about it, which was good, because I didn't know how I could possibly keep that promise anyway. Next we hit a branch of a department store. There wasn't time for me to try anything on, but I was able to pick up some underwear, a nightgown, a couple of tees, and even a little backpack to lug it all around in. We finished off the buying spree with a couple of mango-papaya-coconut smoothies from a Cold Stone

Creamery. We could definitely use one of those where I come from—not that there was a chance in Hell it could happen. Ha-ha; yeah, I know, bad joke.

I'd been a little anxious about being alone with him. I felt perfectly safe, of course, but I was afraid of where the conversation might go. All this lying was making me nervous. I was worried that if he asked me more about my life, where I came from and all that, I'd slip up and contradict myself. Fortunately, we were racing around too much to talk, and even when we were back in the taxi, he didn't ask me any personal questions. He'd picked up a magazine back in the pharmacy, and he was looking at an article.

"Listen to this," he said, and read out loud. "Despite the recent tragic death of her daughter, Margaret Hunsucker remains steadfast in her resolve to become a candidate for president of the United States. She speaks calmly and decisively of the nation's problems and refuses to discuss her own personal grief. She has placed the needs of the American people before her own, and it is only when you peer deeply into her pale-blue eyes that you can see any hint of the sadness she bears."

"Stop," I pleaded. "I may gag."

"I can't believe the hold she has on people," Jordan commented. "This reporter is supposed to be objective, and she's worshipping at Hunsucker's feet. I think this is what creeps me out more than anything, this power she has to make people believe her. It's practically supernatural. Like she's made a pact with the devil or something."

I spent a lot of time taking a very, very long draw on my smoothie. Anything to keep from reacting. Pretty soon I was making those bottom-of-the-empty-cup gurgling sounds and had to stop. Fortunately, by then Jordan had found another disturbing article in the magazine.

"Check it out. According to this article, something like twenty percent of people on death row have IQs below normal. How can they be held responsible for their actions? This isn't right. I want to do something."

"Like the rally you organized for Alton Crenshaw?"

He was startled. "How did you know about that?"

Jeez, was I an idiot. I didn't even need a personal question to get myself into trouble. At least lying was getting easier: "Someone mentioned it last night. Where's the demonstration going to be held today? In front of the White House?"

"No, it's out here in the 'burbs. Some place called the Civic Center. That's where she's speaking."

"Where who's speaking?"

"Who do you think? Margaret Hunsucker."

I sat very, very still and let his words wash over me. I didn't want them to penetrate my ears and register in my brain, but unfortunately, that process just happened naturally. It took me a moment to respond. "She—she's giving a speech?"

"Yeah, that's why we're doing this here, so she can see that she doesn't have the entire country on her side. You didn't know that?"

I shook my head. "I just thought it was a regular demonstration."

"Well, outside, in front of the building, we'll be demonstrating. But a couple of us are going to try to get inside and make a little noise."

I didn't know what to say. This was a complete and total shock, and I wasn't even sure I could identify my feelings. My mother . . . she was going to be there. I might even see her.

Jordan was watching me curiously. "What's the matter? Does it make any difference to you?"

"No," I replied quickly. "Why should it?"

"You look upset."

"I'm just surprised," I said. The understatement of the century.

At least I had some warning now. I could prepare myself not to show whatever I was going to feel when I saw her. And I didn't have to worry about her recognizing me—she'd never seen the results of her birthday gift.

There was more bad news waiting for me back at the hostel, and Ashley couldn't wait to tell me. "Your bed doesn't have a mattress," she said gleefully. "And there are no more beds available."

There was no point in arguing—I could see this for myself. There were four cotlike beds in the tiny room. Ashley and the two other girls from the bus had laid claim to three of them. Mine was just a platform with springs.

I wouldn't give her the satisfaction of seeing my dismay. "I'll manage," I said shortly, and dropped my backpack and bags on the springs. Ashley peered inside one of the bags. "Oh, I see you have new clothes. I thought you didn't have any money."

"Jordan lent me some."

She let out an exaggerated gasp of horror. "You are so using him, aren't you?"

"No," I snapped.

"Then what's the deal? Are you trying to seduce him?"

"*No*. For your information, I live with a guy."

I could see from her expression that she didn't believe me, but I didn't care. All I could think about at this point was finding the shower, brushing my teeth with a real toothbrush, and changing my clothes.

It was so nice to be clean again, to put on clean clothes. And for the first time in ages, I put on some makeup.

I'd never worn much makeup when I was living on

earth. I didn't have anything against the stuff, I just figured no one ever looked at me, so why bother? Lipstick would only draw more attention to my braces, and who'd be able to see shadow and mascara behind my thick glasses? After I got my new look, I was in Hell, and Brad hadn't thought to include cosmetic items in the nice set of toiletries he'd provided for me. Thinking of Brad made me smile. He was the kind of guy who probably never even noticed that women wore makeup.

But while I was in the pharmacy today, I passed through a massive cosmetics section. And though I felt a little guilty spending Jordan's money on nonessential stuff, for some crazy reason I really, really wanted it. I didn't go crazy, I just bought some pink gloss and peachy blush, a liner and mascara for my eyes, plus some shadow. . . . Okay, I did go crazy. As I examined the goodies I'd purchased, I told myself I was only doing this because I needed anything I could get my hands on that might make me feel more confident. Considering that I might have to make eye contact with the woman who had sold me to the devil, I needed all the confidence I could get. But then I remembered that I hadn't known about my mother being there until *after* the shopping. So I really had no excuse at all for my sudden need to beautify. Unless I was trying to impress Jordan. Which, of course, was precisely why I wanted to look good. Wouldn't any girl want to look good around a guy like Jordan? I was only human, sort of.

I stuffed everything into my new backpack, and put it on. I could carry everything around with me, which was good, since I had no intention of leaving my new purchases where Ashley might be able to get her hands on them. Not that I thought she would steal them—I'm sure she thought drugstore brands were beneath her. But I could see her destroying them, just out of spite, because she thought I was into Jordan. She might be a snob, but she wasn't stupid.

By the time I'd finished doing this, it was time to leave for the Civic Center. The bus was waiting for us in front of the hostel. We stuffed signs and a banner in the storage compartment and climbed on. Jordan stood by the door while everyone boarded, and then he got on. He remained standing at the front of the bus and addressed the group.

"Okay, let me tell you how this is going to play." Once again, I was in awe of his power. Fifteen excited, noisy teens went into complete attentive silence the moment he began to speak. I looked around. Nobody seemed the least bit annoyed by his take-charge attitude. He had them all in the palm of his hand.

"We gotta be cool," he began. "No horsing around, no goofing off. I have no idea how many other demonstrators will be there, but we'll probably be the youngest, and we want to blend in and be taken seriously. Hopefully, there will be some media coverage. Don't smile or giggle, or call attention to yourself to get on TV. I'm sure there will be cops, and we don't want to give them any excuse to throw us off the premises. Once things get going, I'm going to scope out the place, see if there's any way of getting inside."

"That's what I want to do," Bayne announced. "If a bunch of us can get inside and we can make enough noise, she won't be able to speak."

Jordan shook his head. "No, man, that's not the plan. We don't want to sound like kids. My idea is that we confront her with questions, and we keep them coming. We try to fluster her, we get her to contradict herself. Let people see that she doesn't know what she's talking about. We're not just trying to make trouble for Hunsucker, we're trying to get more people on our side. So we can't act like idiots, okay? We gotta come across as mature and intelligent."

I could see Bayne's face, and he was the one who now

seemed completely flustered. "How do we do that?" he asked.

"We don't jeer and make noise. We ask solid questions." He grinned. "I just happen to have some right here in my back pocket." He pulled out some small index cards and began distributing them. "If you don't understand your question, just ask me. Practice asking them with each other. Be prepared."

I didn't want a question. Even though I knew my mother couldn't recognize me, I didn't want her eyes on me, I didn't want any kind of connection at all. The very thought made my skin crawl. I knew that was such a cliché, but it was the only way to describe my physical feelings at that moment in time. I was uncomfortable in my own body.

I didn't talk to Jordan at all during the trip. He was our leader, and everyone wanted to be close to him, to ask his advice and get his approval. It was natural, because he was that kind of person. You wanted to be a part of whatever he was a part of. I'd heard of people like this before, who had the force of personality that made others want to follow them. But I never really believed in this kind of power until now.

I wondered if Brad was aware of this, watching it on TV. Could he see Jordan's magnetism? Would he understand what I was feeling right then? I wasn't completely sure I understood it myself. The word that kept echoing in my head was "awe," but I kept thinking there was something else, too. I just hoped I wasn't turning into some kind of groupie.

"There's the Civic Center," the driver called out. From my window I could just make out a large, domed building, with a lot of people gathered in front of it. I could feel the excitement rising in the bus, and I could feel it inside myself, too. This is what I'd come back for, to help stop my mother. I wished I knew from what direction Brad was watching me. I wanted to give him a smile and a thumbs-up.

We ran into a lot of traffic, and it was all moving in the direction of the Civic Center. The bus pulled over to the side of the road, and Jordan announced that we would walk from there. We collected the signs and the banner and made our way over to the center. All the while, I kept looking over my shoulder fearfully, expecting at any moment to see a big black or white or maybe black-*and*-white limousine coming toward us. Or it could be one of those dignified Town Cars, like the kind that picked me up at Woodbridge. Maybe by now my mother had a private helicopter that would place her on the roof of the building. The Civic Center had a domed top, I mused. She'd slide right down.

"What are you smiling about?" Jordan asked.

"Oh, sorry. We're not supposed to smile, are we?"

Jordan laughed. "I just don't want those guys to get goofy. Is this your first demonstration?"

I had a ridiculous desire to invent some sort of personal history of protest marches, but I didn't need to dig myself deeper into fantasyland. "Yes, my very first."

"There's nothing like it to make you feel alive," he said.

Well, that would be helpful, I thought.

"It takes you outside of yourself, beyond your own little world. We're all so trapped in our comfort zones, with family and friends . . . and they're important, too, sure, but we get caught up in trivial problems. When you demonstrate, you confront the fact that there's something more important out there, and you're a part of it."

"I'm glad I'm a part of this," I said.

"So am I."

He was just being nice. And if you're in charge of a demonstration, it would go without saying you'd be glad for anyone to be there. Even so, I couldn't deny the warm, fuzzy feeling his words gave me.

Bayne, walking just ahead of us, turned around. "Hey, Sanders, I don't see any signs."

We were closer now, and the crowd in front of the Civic Center was becoming clearer. I think we all realized something at the same time.

"They're not demonstrators," Jordan said, and I could hear the disappointment in his voice. "They must be here for the speech."

Sure enough, we could see now that the crowd was slowly moving up the steps and inside the building. By the time we reached the steps, there was no one left outside. Except for some police officers. One of them came over to us.

"All right, what do you kids think you're doing here?"

Everyone turned automatically to Jordan. "We want to exercise our right to assembly," Jordan said. "And declare our opposition to the person who's speaking in that building."

"Yeah, yeah, okay," the man said dismissively. He turned to the other cops. "Junior crackpots," he yelled. "Harmless."

"Raise your signs," Jordan called out. Everyone did, and two people unfurled the banner. The cop groaned. "Oh, shit."

"Exactly," Jordan said. "Stop Hunsucker In Time."

"Well, you jerks blew it," the cop declared. "There's a law against vulgarity and obscenity on county property. You want to exercise your fuckin' rights, you gotta do it across the street."

The street happened to be a broad boulevard, which meant that no one coming in or out of the Civic Center would even notice us. Then there was the fact that the entire block on the other side was occupied by an old factory in the process of being demolished. No shops, no businesses—we wouldn't even get interested passersby who might join us.

Jordan didn't seem too dismayed. "All right, folks, you heard the man. Let's cross the street."

But as I started to move in that direction with the others, I felt his hand on my arm. In a low voice, he said, "We're going to get inside the Civic Center."

Once more, I acknowledged his leadership. Even though I had absolutely no desire whatsoever to get any closer to Margaret Hunsucker, I found myself staying by his side. We handed our signs off to others, and moved quickly around to the side of the building, where a line of leafy trees would obscure us. Behind us, I could already hear someone from a passing car yelling at the demonstrators. "You jerks, if you don't love this country, get out!" I felt a little like a traitor, leaving them to the abuse.

But we weren't leaving all of them. "Wait up!" demanded a now-familiar voice. I turned to see Ashley striding toward us.

Jordan shook his head. "Ashley, you don't want to do this with us. We could all get into trouble, and your parents would have a fit. If you stay out here with the others, you'll be okay."

"I don't care, I want to come inside," she said stubbornly. She jerked her head in my direction. "Why should she go with you and not me? I was involved in this before she was."

Jordan looked pained. "Ashley, we're all in this together, it isn't a competition."

Jeez, boys could be so naïve. Then I noticed some movement among the police officers.

"Jordan, if they continue in that direction, they're going to see us," I said in a low tone.

"Keep moving," he muttered. And Ashley moved right along with us. There was a back entrance to the building, but two armed guards stood by it. Jordan strode purposefully toward them, while Ashley and I tried to keep up. Jordan reached in his pocket and pulled out a card.

"Hello, sir, I'm Charles Snodgrass, this is Mary Jane

Murphy, and this is, uh, Ashley Murphy. We're covering the senator's speech for the *Camden Chronicle*."

One of the guards looked at a sheet. "The what?"

"The *Camden High School Daily Chronicle*."

"Oh, yeah, here you are. But there's only supposed to be two of you."

"Yeah, but Ashley here, she's just crazy about the senator, she's been bugging us all week to let her come along, so I was hoping maybe you could bend the rules. . . ." Just then, a couple of guys with a TV camera and a microphone came to the door. As they were showing their credentials, the other guard opened the door and let us in.

"How did you know that name would be on the list?" I asked him in a whisper once we were in the corridor.

"Because I put it there."

"*How?*"

"You wouldn't believe how easy it is to hack into certain public administration files," Jordan told me. Oh, I hoped Brad was watching!

We could hear the murmur of the waiting audience behind a door. Jordan walked on ahead and opened it. Ashley and I were about to enter when we were stopped by a security guard coming out another door off the corridor. He put his hand up to stop us. "Stand back, please."

Jordan looked back at us, mouthed, "I'm going in," and disappeared. Meanwhile, another guard had come out and was standing at attention by the door. A wave of nausea passed over me. I knew what was coming.

The not-so-blessed mother emerged, surrounded on all sides by her flunkies or groupies or whatever. Even though I knew I wouldn't be recognized, I shrank back behind Ashley. And it was a good thing I did, because just behind Margaret

Hunsucker was the one person who *could* recognize me: a petite woman with short, curly blond hair.

Lisa.

I only got a glimpse of her, but that was enough, and I finally understood the expression "my blood ran cold." I started shaking uncontrollably.

The guard ran ahead and opened the door that Jordan had gone through, and the Hunsucker team disappeared.

"C'mon, we can go in now," Ashley said.

"You go," I said. "I'm going back outside."

I didn't know if I was shivering or sweating, but whatever it was must have been pretty dramatic, because even the totally self-absorbed Ashley almost looked concerned.

"What's wrong with you?"

I had no time to answer, and I didn't need to. The door to the auditorium opened again, and Lisa came out, alone. She was looking straight ahead and walking purposefully, and for one brief, hopeful moment I thought she just might not see me. But then she turned, and stopped.

Have you ever watched a horror movie where people see a ghost for the first time? They almost always have the same response. They freeze, and remain very still. The lips part, but no words come out. Next the eyes get bigger. Very slowly, the mouth opens wider and wider and wider. Then comes the ear-piercing scream.

Lisa didn't do any of those things. She just stayed still, watching me carefully, warily, like someone who'd encountered a stranger in a dark alley and was waiting to see if that stranger had bad intentions.

Part of me was ready to turn and run. But another part of me, a bigger part, was expecting something, waiting for something. Maybe not a scream. But at least a little more fear. In any case, the silence was unbearable. I had to break it.

"Hello, Lisa."

I thought I saw her lips move, but I didn't hear anything.

"I'm not a ghost," I said.

I watched her throat jump as she swallowed very hard. "What do you want, Jessica?" she whispered.

"I don't know yet," I replied.

Lisa took two steps backward, and paused. I had a feeling she was testing me, trying to figure out if I had some sort of unearthly powers to kill her in her tracks. When I didn't move, she took another step. Then she quickly turned and ran back into the auditorium.

I wrapped my arms around myself and shivered with cold. At the same time, I felt the beads of sweat trickle down from my forehead. I couldn't move. I don't know how long I stayed like this, not seeing or hearing or even thinking. Then, out of the corner of my eye, I saw Ashley. She spoke.

"What was *that* all about?"

Chapter
Sixteen

"**N**OTHING," I REPLIED, and started walking. Ashley stayed by my side.

"She knew you."

"No, she didn't," I said.

"Well, you knew *her*."

"No, I didn't."

"You called her by name! You said, 'Hello, Lisa.'"

"Lucky guess."

"But she didn't call you Janie. She called you something else."

"Exactly. It was a case of mistaken identity." I picked up my pace and left her behind.

The protest was still in place across the street from the Civic Center entrance, walking back and forth, but the group was moving slowly, and the chanting was pretty lethargic. I could see why. No one had joined them, no one was watching. They weren't even getting any more jeers. They were performing for an empty house. Even the cops seemed to have drifted away.

A couple of kids had given up, and were sitting on the curb. "Anyone get inside?" Bayne asked as I approached.

"Only Jordan," I replied. I picked up Bayne's sign and

joined the shuffling demonstrators. I saw Ashley go up to Bayne, and I could tell she was talking excitedly. I didn't need to hear her to know what she was talking about.

Now that the shock of seeing my mother and Lisa had waned, I could start planning how to explain all this to Jordan when Ashley informed him of the encounter. I wasn't too worried. From what Jordan said and the way he acted, I assumed he thought Ashley was just a kid, and he wouldn't take anything she said too seriously. I hoped it wouldn't be hard for me to convince him that she'd misunderstood what she saw.

One thing I could say favorably about Margaret Hunsucker—the woman had stamina. She managed to keep those folks inside entertained for almost two hours. By the time the fans started to emerge from the Civic Center, we were pretty much wrecked.

Of course, Jordan, being Jordan, didn't look tired at all when he joined us, but he wasn't happy, either. "I couldn't get called on," he told us when we all gathered around him. "The jerks on the stage, they wouldn't look at me. I even tried to act like a stupid high-school kid, waving my hands and jumping up and down—I figured they might think it was media-worthy. You know, the younger generation and all that crap. I might as well have been invisible."

"What did Hunsucker talk about?" one of the guys asked.

"Usual BS. Americans deserve peace and prosperity, blah blah blah. Anything happen out here?"

"Naw, it was dead," the guy reported. "I think we can write this day off."

"Not so fast," Bayne said. "Wait till you hear what my kid sister learned."

Ashley and Bayne must have planned this preamble to the news, I thought. Ashley was taking full advantage of the dramatic introduction. She pushed herself to the front of the group, stood by Jordan, and pointed a finger at guess who.

"You might want to ask your new friend here exactly whose side she's on."

I wanted Jordan to look at me so we could share a little eye-roll, but Ashley had his attention. "What are you talking about, Ash?"

"She's all buddy-buddy with a woman on Hunsucker's staff! I saw her. They were talking to each other like old friends!"

I was gratified to see that Jordan's expression was highly skeptical. But her brother had something to add.

"It sounds like something Hunsucker would do, right, Sanders? Send out followers to check up on any opposition?"

"This is ridiculous," I fumed.

"You knew each other," Ashley declared.

"It was a mistake."

"Then how did you know her name?" Ashley challenged. "You said, 'Hello, Lisa.'"

"She looked like someone I knew, someone named Lisa. Maybe her name was Lisa, too, it's a common name." I tried another tactic. "Ashley, even if that woman knew me, which she didn't, but even if she did, how could you think that I'm a spy? Did that woman look happy to see me?"

"Of course she wasn't happy," Ashley countered. "You were supposed to be out here, spying on us, not in there, watching your leader!" She turned to Jordan, and her face went all sweetsy-cutesy. "You believe me, don't you, Jordan? I would never lie to you."

By now, our bus had pulled up to the curb, and the driver was motioning to us. Jordan put a hand to his head and rubbed his forehead. "Ashley, I'm not calling you a liar, but you might have misinterpreted this. Look, we're all wiped out. Let's go back to the hostel and get something to eat."

I hung back and let the others get on first. I needed to talk to Jordan, even though I wasn't sure what I was going to say. It was pretty creepy—people were shooting me dubious looks as they passed. Ashley lingered, too, watching me suspiciously. Jordan didn't say anything, but he put a hand lightly on my shoulder and propelled me toward the bus. Ashley was in the process of going up the steps when she stopped suddenly and turned around.

"I just remembered what that woman called you. Jessica. Is that your real name?"

I felt Jordan's hand tighten on my shoulder. "Get on the bus, Ashley" was all he said.

We followed her. I took a seat by a window, and Jordan sat down next to me. I was trying to come up with some kind of story, but just as I opened my mouth, Jordan put a finger to his.

"Not here. Let's talk when we get back."

Pretending to doze, I leaned back in my seat and closed my eyes. My creative skills kicked into high gear, and a story began to form.

I knew who Lisa was because . . . because Jessica Hunsucker had sent me some pictures of the campaign staff, and Lisa was in a photo. And she called me Jessica because . . . because Jessica and I looked alike when we were in kindergarten, people used to say we were like twins, and we called ourselves Jessica One and Jessica Two, and Jessica must have told Lisa about this and shown her a photo of us then and me now, and . . . no, this was getting too complicated.

The name Jessica was the number-one name for girls in the United States the year I was born. I knew this was a fact— I'd looked it up once. People could easily know two or three

Jessicas my age. Lisa simply mistook me for some other Jessica she knew. Not Jessica Hunsucker.

Back at the hostel, Jordan handed Bayne a bunch of bills and told everyone to go to the cafeteria on the ground floor. "I'll be with you in a minute," he told them. He didn't say anything about me, but he took my hand, and it was clear I was meant to stay behind.

"We have to talk," he said.

His voice was calm and gentle, and his grip on my hand wasn't strong. I didn't feel trapped, and I knew I could have pulled free and run. But I didn't. Without speaking, we climbed a couple of flights of stairs and went down a hallway.

Jordan took out a key and unlocked a room. It wasn't luxurious, but it had to be one of the better hostel rooms—there were two beds instead of four, and a chair. Jordan pointed to it, and I sat down. Jordan sat on the edge of the bed, and regarded me intently.

"What's the story?" he asked.

I took a breath, and opened my mouth. And at that split second, I made a decision.

"Jordan . . . do you believe in an afterlife?"

He didn't appear to be startled by the question. His gaze remained steady, and he seemed to be considering an answer.

"I'm not religious," he said finally.

"But do you think the notion of something after death is completely insane?"

"No," he replied. "Not *completely*." He paused. "You did know that woman, didn't you? And she knew you."

I nodded.

"Because . . . ?"

It was remarkable, how easily the words came out. "Because I'm Jessica Hunsucker."

He didn't smile, he didn't frown, his eyebrows didn't go

up. Did he think I was a lunatic whom he'd have to pacify until he could contact the men in white coats? Was there still time for me to laugh it off and pretend this was all a great big put-on?

To my surprise, he nodded. "You said something about how Hunsucker might have planned her daughter's kidnapping and murder to get sympathy votes. I'm guessing you escaped, changed your appearance . . . right?"

If I'd been enthralled with him before, I was now in awe. He was so close. Now I knew I could tell him the real story.

"Before I was born, she made a deal with the devil, to give him her child in exchange for political power. And on my sixteenth birthday, he sent a demon to pick me up and take me to Hell. That's where I've been for the past couple of weeks. But the demon let me come back to earth, so I could try to stop my mother from becoming president."

"So you really are the girl I saw in front of Woodbridge. Which was why you knew about my Alton Crenshaw demonstration."

I nodded.

"You did a good job changing your appearance. I didn't recognize you at all."

"My mother's birthday gift. A makeover. I thought it was a pretty cool gift at the time. But she only wanted to make sure no one would recognize me if I got away from the demon."

"Did you see her today? Did *she* see you?"

"I saw her pass, but even if she saw me, she wouldn't recognize me. I never saw her after the makeover. Lisa was with me that day; she'd be the only person who would know me."

"Lisa. The woman Ashley saw you talking with."

"Yes. My mother's personal assistant. She was in on the whole thing. When we got back to the house that afternoon, she put something in my tea, and I passed out in my room. When I woke up, the demon was there."

Jordan leaned forward, resting his elbows on his knees and folding his hands. He stared at the floor. I stared at his hands.

They were big, and they looked strong. Smooth, too. No nasty calluses. His fingernails were clean, and I could see he didn't bite his nails or pick at his cuticles. I liked the way the golden hairs gave a little shimmer to his tan. How did he keep that tan, anyway? It was November. I didn't think he was the type to go to tanning salons—he didn't seem vain.

And why were these irrelevant thoughts filling my head? Because he was deep in thought, and I didn't want to imagine what he might be thinking.

Finally, he looked up. "And this demon—he let you go?"

"Yes."

"Sounds like an awfully nice guy. For a demon, I mean."

"Oh, he is," I assured him. "Brad's terrific, he's a good person, he's in Hell because he did something stupid. It's a long story—"

He interrupted. "Your demon's name is Brad?"

"Bradley George Cameron."

"Cameron," he repeated. "Isn't that what you're calling yourself? Janie Cameron."

I nodded.

"So—are you two, like, married or something? Are you a demon, too?"

"Oh, no," I said quickly. "I just needed a name." Briefly, I wondered if I'd insulted Brad with my denial. Maybe I should have tugged on my earlobe before I answered. But we weren't married, and I didn't want to go into the whole partner-mate thing.

"And I'm not a demon," I added. "I'm just a regular, you

know . . ." I hesitated. What were we called, the ordinary citizens of Hell?

"Inmate?" Jordan suggested. "Prisoner?" He almost smiled. "I can't believe you'd be classified as a sinner."

"Resident," I said. "That's what I am. And you know, it's really not that terrible. I mean, it's no theme park, but there's a Red Lobster, and we might be getting a Starbucks . . . and we can watch life on earth. That's how I found out about my mother's plans." I told him about the memo.

He rubbed his forehead again, as if he were forcing the incredible information into his mind. Or maybe I was just giving him a headache.

"Jordan? Do you believe me?"

His eyes returned to me. "Yes, I believe you." He meant that, too, I could tell. Relief came over me, covered me like a soft, warm, comforting blanket. For the first time since I came back to earth, I felt almost safe.

"There's something you have to do, Jessica," he said.

It was lovely, hearing him say my real name. "What?"

"You have to contact this Lisa person. And tell her you want to see your mother."

Seventeen

I WAITED for the punch line. It didn't come. "What?" I asked again, but in a different tone this time.

"Don't you see? This is our big chance."

"Our big chance for"—I hated saying it again, but there was no other word—"*what*?"

He jumped off the bed and began pacing the room. I could see he was getting excited. "It could work, Jessica, it could really work. You talk to Lisa and you force her to set it up. You threaten Lisa with going public about your mother selling you to the devil unless she organizes a private meeting."

"Oh, come on, Jordan. She'll just laugh. She has to know people won't buy a story like that."

"You don't think so? They're buying Margaret Hunsucker's stories on how she's going to turn the world around. And was Lisa laughing when she saw you today?"

"No."

"How did she look?"

I thought back. "Scared. No . . . nervous."

"Exactly. Maybe she won't think people will believe the devil story. But she doesn't know that for sure. And I'll bet she wouldn't want to take the chance."

"And then what?" I asked him. "I get this meeting. And

I threaten my mother with the same thing? Tell her I'll go public with this story unless she pulls out of the race?" I shook my head. "You don't know Margaret Hunsucker, Jordan. She is a very strong woman. And if you haven't figured this out by now, she's got very good connections. We could all end up down under, and I'm not talking about Australia."

He shook his head. "No, you're not going to threaten *her*. Like you said, she wouldn't pull out. Even if she did, her fans would go ballistic, they'd rise up and organize. She'd become a write-in candidate and she'd still win. No, what you have to do is get her to admit to her schemes, what she really wants to do. All that stuff about causing revolutions in other countries, getting rid of all the poor people, deporting them or exterminating them, whatever she's got planned. You get her to say these things out loud. And you'll get it all on tape."

"On tape," I repeated.

"We'll get you wired, you'll have some sort of recorder on you. And I'll figure out a way to put a transmitter on you, so I can be listening in and recording it back here, too. Just in case you get caught and your recorder is discovered."

"Oh, thanks a lot," I said sarcastically. "But I'll be the only one in real danger. You know what kind of woman my mother is. She's willing to do anything to get her way. To anyone. Including her daughter."

"Yeah, but what can she do to you? What can anyone do to you? You're already dead, right?"

I didn't feel like getting into the whole dead/not-dead thing with him right then. I just shook my head.

"I can't do it, I can't. I won't face that woman. You can't possibly understand how I feel about her. It's beyond hate, Jordan. Just getting that glimpse of her today . . ." I was becoming nauseated again, remembering the moment. "If I have to be close to her, if I have to hear her voice again, I don't know, it's—it's like something would happen to me, I wouldn't be the same, I couldn't bear it. . . ." I could hear my voice rising, pleading.

Jordan sat back down on the edge of the bed, facing me. He took my hands in his.

"You could save the world," he said simply.

But what about *me*? I wanted to scream. Hadn't I been through enough? Did I really have to suffer more?

My eyes were burning, and I looked down. My small hands had disappeared inside Jordan's. I could feel my own palms clasped together, clammy and hot, but his were soft and cool.

So was his voice. "You've been given this amazing opportunity, Jessica. Think of what you'd be doing for people, for your country. Once this tape is played on CNN and the nation hears what she's really all about, well . . . her supporters may be stupid, but they're not necessarily evil. They won't back ideas like hers."

I raised my eyes and looked beseechingly into his.

"You could stop her, Jessica. Isn't that what you came back for?"

I gave what I'm sure was an imperceptible nod, but I could see he was encouraged.

"You know, Jessica, most people lead insignificant lives. Not because they want to—they just don't get the chance to do something grand, something that could make an impact. You've got that chance."

"I'm frightened," I whispered, and immediately wanted to kick myself for saying that. I'd been doing some pretty wild stuff lately, and here I was sounding like some whiny little wimp.

But Jordan understood. "I know," he said. "I don't blame you. But think about this. She can't hurt you any more than she already has. And I don't know if you're into revenge, but you'll be getting a crack at that, too." He took a cell phone out of his pocket. "Call Lisa."

I took the phone in my hand, but I didn't do anything with it. "I don't know her phone number," I said. "I don't even know her last name."

Jordan got up and went to his suitcase. Opening it, he extracted a small notebook computer.

"I hope they have Wi-Fi in this building," he muttered.

They did. He got online, Googled "Margaret Hunsucker campaign headquarters," and went to the Web site. "Staff . . . ," he read aloud. "Campaign director, executive secretary, press liaison . . . here she is. Personal assistant, Lisa Larkin. And here's the number." He pointed to the screen. "Want me to dial it for you?"

"I can dial it," I said. I was feeling strangely calm now. Maybe it was from being around Jordan, maybe I was absorbing his confidence. I thought about Brad, watching. Was he feeling proud of me right now, with what I was about to do? I punched in the numbers, held the phone to my ear, and listened to the ring. Maybe she wouldn't be there, or I'd just get a machine.

"Hunsucker Headquarters," a perky voice chirped. "How can I help you?"

My voice was surprisingly steady. "I'd like to speak with Lisa Larkin, please."

"May I ask who's calling, please?"

I was tempted to say Madeline, or Monica, or Marla, one of the names Lisa had given me when I was getting my eyes fixed and my braces off and my hair colored. But she might not have my excellent memory.

"Just tell her it's Jessica. I'm an old friend, she'll know who it is." And for once, I was truly grateful to have such a common name. This woman on the phone wouldn't make any connection between this caller and the senator's late daughter.

But Lisa did. I could hear the tremor in her voice when she spoke into the phone. "This is Lisa Larkin."

"Hello, Lisa. Do you know who this is?"

There was the briefest possible hesitation, and then a grudging yes.

"I can tell you what I want now."

She didn't respond, but I could hear her breathing. I went on. "I want to see my mother."

This time there was no hesitation. "No. That's not possible."

"Anything's possible, Lisa. I'm the proof of that. You know, back from the dead. . . ." I looked at Jordan. He smiled broadly and made a thumbs-up gesture.

"She won't agree to this," Lisa said.

"Then you'll have to talk her into it," I replied. "And remember, Lisa, I have connections now, too. You know what I mean. Fire and brimstone . . ."

I could just make out a slight choking sound on the other end of the line. I went on.

"See what you can do, Lisa. I'd like to meet tomorrow morning. You can reach me at this number." I glanced toward Jordan and raised my eyebrows. He recited the digits, and I repeated them.

"Who's with you?" Lisa asked sharply.

"I don't think you really want to know that, Lisa," I said. "I'll be expecting your call." I hit the red "off" button, and looked at Jordan. "I kind of enjoyed that."

"You were great!" Jordan exclaimed. He practically lifted me off the chair and hugged me.

"It's not really like that, you know," I said when he released me. "I haven't seen any fire and brimstone."

"That's good to know," he said. "Just in case I end up there, too."

"I can't imagine that happening to you," I said. "You're too good."

"Hey, you're going to make me blush," he said.

Would a blush show through that tan? I wondered. Then I was thinking about his chest. Would the golden hairs shimmer there, too, like they did on his hands? I had this crazy, almost voracious desire to know. That brief hug he'd just given me—I could still feel it. I wanted to feel it more.

Was he mind-reading? He was watching me now, with a different expression.

"Are you really dead?" he asked.

"It's a long story," I said.

And then I knew it was time to tug on my earlobe.

chapter
Eighteen

IT WASN'T my first time, physically, but it was the first time with feeling, so it was a new experience. All I really remembered about the leadership-camp event was a lot of fumbling and groping. This time—okay, I don't want to make it sound like some sort of "I floated away on clouds of passion and ecstasy" state of mind. But most of it was pretty damned amazing.

It wasn't even awkward. I felt safe and secure, and everything seemed natural and normal. And exciting, too. I can't go into details. Reading about stuff like this in teen novels always made me cringe with embarrassment. But I will say this—afterward, I was completely drained. Blissful, too. I felt so—so desirable, so beautiful. I looked at his face—maybe it was just being with someone so good-looking that made me feel pretty hot myself, I don't know. I didn't care why I felt like this. I only wanted to go on feeling this way.

But nothing lasts forever. As I lay there beside him, with the blanket pulled over us and only our hands touching underneath it, there was a knock on the door.

"Jordan? Are you in there?"

Even through the heavy door I recognized Ashley's nasal, whiny voice. So did Jordan. He put a finger to his lips, and I figured we'd just pretend there was no one here. Then he winced.

"I didn't lock the door," he whispered. In a louder voice, he yelled, "Hold on, I'm coming." He leaped out of bed and pulled on his jeans. Barefoot, and bare-chested, he went to the door and opened it just wide enough to slip out. I could have sworn I heard Ashley's swift intake of breath when she beheld the half-naked Jordan.

"Just wondering what you were up to," she told him. "Some of us are going into D.C. to hang out in Georgetown, see if we can find some club that will let us in. Are you coming?"

"Gee, Ashley, I don't think so, I'm really tired. In fact, I was just getting ready for a little siesta. You guys go on, have fun, we'll touch base later."

Ashley apparently was in no rush to join the group. "By the way, have you seen the spy?" Ashley continued.

"Who?"

"Janie, or Jessica, or whatever her name is. I think she's disappeared. Which is a good thing, in my opinion."

"I don't know where she is," Jordan replied. "Listen, I'm beat, okay?"

"C'mon, Jordan, you haven't even eaten," she wheedled. "And you deserve a little fun, you can't be a radical militant rebel leader all the time."

I heard him laugh, and then I heard something that sounded suspiciously like a kiss—but I assumed it was on her cheek.

"Thanks, babe, you're probably right, but I really need to crash. I'll see you guys later."

I could still hear her protests as he closed the door.

"Hungry?" he asked me as he climbed back into bed.

I realized it was dark out, and it had to be at least eight. I hadn't thought about food till he asked, but I answered promptly. "Starving."

"Let's see what delivers around here." He went to his laptop and started typing. "Hey, do you have wireless in Hell?"

"I don't think so. I could ask Brad—he's a high-tech kind of guy."

"Brad's the demon, right?"

I knew Brad wasn't watching us, but even so, I felt uncomfortable. "Jordan, let's not talk about Hell, okay? I'd rather just talk about, you know . . . now."

Jordan flashed me his brilliant smile. "That's fine with me. You like pepperoni?" He picked up his phone and called in an order. When he was finished, he kept looking at the phone screen.

"There's a text message," he said.

I sat up. "For you?"

He hit a button and looked at the screen for another couple of seconds. "No. I think this is for you." He handed me the phone. The message was short and to the point.

Tomorrow. Noon. Pelham & Oak.

I assumed that Pelham and Oak were the names of streets, and that I'd be meeting Margaret Hunsucker where they intersected. Now that an actual time and place had been set, I started feeling very vulnerable again. Being naked didn't help, especially since Jordan still had his jeans on.

"I think I'll put something on," I murmured.

Jordan had gone back to his laptop. "I'll do a MapQuest. Pelham and Oak . . ."

From the backpack, I pulled out the brand-new nightie I'd picked up today. This was no flannel-and-flower gown like I'd been wearing in Hell. This little thing was black, with thin straps and a little lace around the bust. And it came to just above my knees. In terms of actual clothing, it wasn't much, but I did feel a little more in control than I did when I was completely naked.

I joined Jordan at the computer.

"We can't print this out, but it doesn't look too complicated," Jordan said. He started going through the directions that would get me from the hostel to the meeting point. "Looks like it could be within walking distance."

"That's good," I said. I busied myself making up the bed. A few minutes later, there was another knock on the door. This time it was the pizza delivery man. Jordan paid him, took the box, placed it on the bed, and opened it. A tantalizing and very familiar scent filled the air. I remembered that I'd had a pepperoni pizza just a few days ago.

With Brad.

This is my food thing: I like to eat. I eat when I'm happy, I eat when I'm depressed. The only time I don't want to eat is when I'm feeling confused, nervous, conflicted, jumpy— and guilty. This pizza looked great, smelled great, and probably tasted great, but I'd completely lost my appetite. I suppose one reason was the text message I'd just received. But another reason was Brad.

Why was I feeling guilty? Because just a few days ago I was ready to go to bed with *him*? How silly of me. Okay, so I was supposed to be Brad's "mate," by the laws of Hell. But I hadn't signed anything. We hadn't made any sort of pledge to each other. Sure, he was a nice guy, and he'd been kind to me, but I didn't owe him anything for this, did I?

And it wasn't like he'd *seen* me and Jordan and I'd hurt his feelings. He'd said he would turn off the TV when I tugged on my earlobe, and I'm sure he did, because he was the kind of person who kept his word.

But . . . what if he missed my earlobe tug? What if Brad

had just witnessed my—what Jordan and I did? I still had absolutely no reason to feel guilty, did I? I wasn't madly in love with Jordan or anything like that. It was just a massive crush, like the kind you might have for any Justin or Ashton or whoever your ideal guy might be. It wasn't like it meant anything. And I had to take into account the circumstances. I was feeling fragile, I knew I was going to have to confront my mother, I was tense. I was in an unusual state.

Yeah. Like I wasn't freaking out when I found myself stranded in Hell—and that didn't drive me into Brad's arms. But—*hello???*—Brad's a demon. Brad's *dead.* Jordan's . . . so alive.

"Aren't you going to eat anything?" Jordan asked me. While I was lost in all my crazy thoughts, he'd managed to devour half the pizza.

"I'm nervous," I replied.

"Yeah, this can't be easy for you," he said. "But I want you to start thinking about the meeting. What you're going to say, how you're going to get her to admit to her plans and say it out loud."

"Right."

"I've got some ideas on how you could approach her."

I tried to concentrate on what he was saying, but I was annoyed to find that my mind kept turning back to Brad. That sweet, anxious, eager-to-please expression—it was funny how I'd actually begun to find him appealing. But that was before Jordan.

Ohmigod. Maybe I *was* falling in love. But who with?

"What do you think?" Jordan asked.

"Hm?"

"You know her better than I do. Which approach would work? Should you tell her what you know about her plans? There's a chance she'd just deny it. Or should you ask her exactly what she's going to do as president? You could even say that living in Hell has changed you, that you appreciate evil now, and that might encourage her to open up."

"I'm not sure."

Jordan finished his slice. "Well, think about it. I'm going to take a shower."

He left the room. I picked up a slice of pizza and tried to recall exactly what I'd been thinking about. Right, the possibility that I was falling in love with Jordan. Well, that was a nonstarter—it wasn't like we could have a lasting relationship. I mean, what would happen when I went back to Hell? Did I actually think he'd follow me there?

If I went back to Hell.

It was a stupid notion, not even worth contemplating. I didn't have any choice in the matter. I had to go back. Whenever Brad decided the time was right, he would come to earth and get me. And I wouldn't be able to hide from him now, any more than I'd been able to hide from him the night he first came to collect me. He wasn't a regular, ordinary guy, he was a demon, he had powers. He'd find me.

But maybe this wouldn't have to happen anytime soon. I had work to do here, and Brad knew that. Talking to my mother tomorrow was only the beginning. I'd have to stick around to keep my eye on her, wouldn't I?

Then I had another idea. Something Jordan had said about pretending that Hell had turned me into a sinner. . . . What if I could really convince her of that? Maybe she'd want to keep me here, working with her on her campaign. There was always the possibility that I wouldn't be able to get her to admit to anything tomorrow. But if I went to work for her, I'd be able to get my hands on the memo, get some evidence of her goals. And then I could really have an impact!

I couldn't wait to tell Jordan this idea. But when he

returned from the shower, damp and golden, with a towel wrapped around his waist, my thoughts shifted.

Oh, my. I dropped my slice of pizza and got up. But before I could reach him, his phone rang and he picked it up.

"Yeah? Right. Okay." He dropped the phone and started to dress.

"What are you doing?" I'd already pulled my T-shirt over my head.

"I'm going to meet the others," he said.

"Now?" I asked in dismay.

"It's okay, you don't have to come." He grinned. "Maybe it's better if you don't. Ashley's probably got them all worked up and ready for a lynching."

I wished I'd had more practice in striking seductive poses. "Do you really have to go?"

"I need to give them something to do for tomorrow. Since we have to stay overnight, we might as well try to accomplish something here."

Personally, I felt like he and I had accomplished quite a bit already. But Jordan's mind was on higher things.

"I'll get them started on making up a flyer," he said. "There's gotta be a copy shop around here somewhere. Then they can team up and go to the tourist sights in the morning to distribute them." He planted a kiss on my forehead, and then he was out the door.

I fell back on the bed. *Damn*. Then something else dawned on me. Back in Hell, Brad and I had worked up a signal that would alert him to turn off the TV. But we'd never come up with any way for me to let him know it was okay to turn it back on. Would he wait till the next morning? That wouldn't be too fabulous. I had every intention of spending the night here and waking up in Jordan's arms.

I hated the thought of hurting Brad's feelings. But he'd

probably find out about me and Jordan sooner or later anyway. It could be for the best. Maybe he wouldn't want me back. . . . I shivered. And what then? I'd simply be assigned to another demon. One who could very well be a lot more demonic.

I closed my eyes. I really didn't want to think about any of this. I wished Jordan would come back.

I'd better get used to his being away a lot, though, because I was sure this was how it was going to be. A revolutionary's life just wasn't his own, and my life with this particular agitator wouldn't be private. I thought about women in the past who must have had to deal with this kind of situation, women who were in love with great men. Coretta Scott King. Josephine Bonaparte. I didn't know if there had been a Mrs. Che Guevara, but if there was, I'm sure she didn't have an easy time of it. And what about poor Mary Magdalene? I'll bet she wasn't thrilled every time Jesus took off to give his sermons on the mounts. Not that I was comparing Jordan to Jesus. . . .

That was when I must have fallen asleep, because I dreamed that Jordan walked on water.

I woke to the sound of the door opening. I was also aware that daylight was streaming into the room.

"Hey, Sleeping Beauty."

I struggled to a sitting position. "What time is it?" I asked groggily.

"Almost ten. You were asleep when I got back. Then I had to run out and pick up some stuff for you." He opened the bag he was carrying. "A recorder, some tape . . ." He grinned. "By the way, Ashley's been telling everyone you didn't sleep in your bed last night."

"How could I? There was no mattress!"

"Don't worry. I told them I found you another room. Then they were shocked because I was aiding and abetting the enemy. So I had to tell them you were helping out today."

"Jordan! You didn't tell them who I am, did you?"

"No, of course not," he hastily assured me. "I just told them you had a connection through that woman, Lisa. And you've got a meeting with Margaret Hunsucker today. They're pretty excited." He sat down on the bed. "How are *you* feeling?"

"Not excited."

"It's going to be okay. We're going to practice this. Let's get you into Mata Hari mode first."

I doubt that Mata Hari wore jeans, but once Jordan began adjusting the recording device around my waist, I definitely began to feel a little spyish. When I put my T-shirt on over it, it couldn't be seen at all. Then we tested it. Facing Jordan, I put a hand on my waist, felt the button, and turned it on.

"Testing, one, two, three," Jordan said. "Jessica Hunsucker is one hot chick."

I laughed. Then I pulled my shirt up, hit the rewind and then the playback. "Testing, one, two, three. Jessica Hunsucker is one hot chick." It was perfectly clear. You could even hear my giggles.

"Now, let's rehearse this," Jordan said. "You're you, I'm your mother." He spoke in a higher-pitched voice. "Hello, Jessica, dear. You're looking very well. I love your hair like that."

I cracked up. "Jordan, this is a woman who sold her daughter to the devil. I don't think she'd greet me like that."

"I was just trying to get you to relax. You're looking pretty tense."

"Can you blame me?"

He turned serious. "No, not at all. Okay, you know her better than I do. You tell me what she'll say when she sees you."

I didn't have the slightest idea. Jordan was wrong. We were talking about a woman I never knew at all.

Nineteen

I WAS GETTING used to the feel of the recording device taped to my waist. I began to worry that I'd forget it was there.

"Remind me to turn on the recorder," I said to Jordan. "When she comes, cough or something."

"I won't be there," Jordan replied. I turned to him with a look of alarm, and he put a comforting arm around my shoulders. "Jessica, you know she won't talk if someone else is there. It's got to be just you and her, alone."

"Where will you be?"

"Not far away. Don't worry. I'll know what's going on."

What could I say? I had to trust him.

He checked the directions he'd copied down from MapQuest. "We make a left here, on Oak. We should hit Pelham in two blocks." He must have sensed my rising anxiety level, because he hugged me tighter. Then he removed his arm from my shoulder and took my hand.

"You can do this, Jessica. You've been to Hell and back. Literally. You're strong, you're smart. It'll come to you, what you need to say to her." He squeezed my hand. "I promise you, everything will be all right."

We'd almost reached the second corner. "I'm going to

leave you here," he said. "We don't want to run the risk of her seeing me."

"What time is it?" I asked.

"Five to twelve. Do you know any breathing exercises?"

"What?"

"Like they do in yoga. For relaxing."

Wow, he was into yoga. Could he be any more perfect?

I smiled. "I'll be okay."

We were face to face. He put a hand on my chin and raised my head. Then he kissed me, and not just a peck, but a real kiss on the mouth. And then he was gone.

Oak was a quiet, leafy boulevard, wide, with a green strip of grass running down the middle and dividing the two directions. There were benches on the grass, at regular intervals. I crossed over and sat down on the one closest to Pelham Street.

I didn't know any breathing exercises. The only kind I'd ever seen was the birth scene in a movie they showed us in sex-ed class. The woman was panting, with short, hard gasps. I didn't think that was the right kind of breathing for this situation.

I was almost glad I'd had that glimpse of my mother yesterday. The first shock was over. I'd be able to handle this better. Would she know me? I wondered. Surely Lisa had prepped her about my new look.

It seemed like more than five minutes had passed. Maybe this was all a hoax, just to get me off her back. Or a setup. Was I about to be kidnapped?

Jordan had said he would know what was going on. Did that mean he could see me right now? And what about Brad—had he turned the TV back on? I hoped that he was watching—and that he'd started watching *after* the kiss.

A few cars had passed by, going pretty fast on this empty

boulevard. The car that was turning onto Oak now was moving slower. It wasn't a limo, or even a luxury car. Just an ordinary, midsize vehicle. Very discreet. I could make out a figure driving. There didn't seem to be anyone else in the car.

The driver came to a stop. I put my hand on my waist, and felt for the "record" button on the device. Then I folded my hands and rested them in my lap—probably to keep them from shaking.

The door opened, and she got out.

Only the size and shape gave any indication it was her. An elaborately tied pale-blue scarf hid the dark-blond hair, and her face was half covered by enormous sunglasses. I couldn't even tell if she was looking at me. It was a good camouflage. Anyone passing by wouldn't look twice at this woman.

She wore a long trench coat, and both her hands were in the deep pockets. I tensed up. Was she about to pull out a pistol? My mind was racing. What would a bullet do to me? Would it hurt?

The sound of the shot was heart-stopping. I'd never heard anything so loud in my life.

My mother's hands were still in her pockets. But her scarf was red now. And before my eyes, Margaret Hunsucker crumpled to the ground.

chapter
Twenty

I COULDN'T MOVE. I remained precisely where I was, sitting on the bench, my hands folded, my eyes on Margaret Hunsucker. The red color of the scarf began to spread, and seeped into crevices of the pavement. I watched in a state of frozen fascination as a trickle of blood traveled into the green part of the divider and disappeared in the grass.

I wondered if I should go to her. She could still be alive, I supposed. But in that position, and with all that blood, it didn't seem very likely. Strange, how logically I was thinking. I'd just seen a murder take place; why wasn't I hysterical? Shouldn't I be screaming or something? Looking back now, I guess I was in shock.

Others had heard the shot. Doors began to open, and some people came out onto their porches. I could hear shouts, loud gasps, but no one ran toward the body. I couldn't blame them—the shooter might still be around somewhere. So why wasn't I running from the scene? Why wasn't I in fear of a random sniper?

Someone must have called 911. I could hear sirens in the distance getting louder, and at that point I actually began to feel something. Panic. I had to get away, run, hide from the police.

Then logic, or whatever had been keeping me calm, took over again. Why should I run? I was sitting here on a bench, with no weapon, and from the way she had fallen, there was no indication she had been heading in my direction. Nobody could connect me with the woman lying there. I had nothing to do with this, I was an innocent bystander.

An ambulance followed by four police cars arrived, and I watched the ensuing scene. A couple of cops jumped out of one car with their guns drawn. Two guys in white ran to the body on the ground. One took the woman's hand, another put two fingers on her neck. Checking for a pulse, I presumed. One of them must have removed her dark glasses, because I heard voices rise and become more excited in tone. I couldn't hear exactly what they were saying, but I had a feeling she'd been recognized.

A cop was headed in my direction. He whipped a pad out of his pocket and jotted something down. "Your name?"

"J-Janie." What was my last name? "Cameron. Sorry, I'm a little shook up."

"Did you see what happened?"

"I heard a shot. I saw her fall."

"But you didn't see a shooter."

"No."

"Could you tell what direction the shot came from?"

"No."

His voice became more gentle. "Are you okay?"

"Yes."

"You sure? This had to be traumatic for you. You could be in shock. I'll get a paramedic over here."

"No, no, thank you. I'm okay, really."

A policewoman joined us. "From the angle of entry, it doesn't look like the killer was on this street or in one of these houses. I'd say the bullet came from there." She pointed in the direction of what looked like an apartment building, just behind a house. "My guess is that he was on the roof, with a long-range rifle."

"You got the building surrounded?" the other cop asked.

"Yeah, but he's probably long gone by now. We've got a team going up to see what he might have left behind. Who's this?" She was looking at me now.

"Cameron, Jane. She heard the shot, saw the woman drop, that's all." To me, he added, "You'll have to come back to the station with us and make a report." I nodded.

Then they lost interest in me and talked to each other. I looked back to where a yellow strip was now being dragged around the spot where she fell. The victim was on a stretcher, lifted by two of the people in white. Another joined them, and put a sheet over her, covering her completely. I watched as the sheet went over her face, and then I knew for sure.

Margaret Hunsucker was dead. My mother was dead.

Had my expression revealed something? The female cop was now looking at me curiously. "Did you know her?" she asked, pointing to the stretcher.

"No."

I wasn't sure how long I sat there. The ambulance took off. Police were still going from house to house, talking to people, probably trying to find out if there had been witnesses other than me. Others had joined them and were scouring the ground where she fell. More cops were inside the car she'd driven there.

A truck bearing letters that looked like a logo for a TV station approached. At the same time, from the other direction, an ordinary car slowed down just in front of me.

"Jessica!"

Jordan was in the driver's seat. Finally, my body began to obey the orders from my brain. I got up and went to the car.

"I'm supposed to go to the police station," I told him.

"Get in," he said.

I did, and he pulled away.

"I know what happened," he said. "I heard it on the radio."

"Whose car is this?" I asked.

"I rented it. The bus is leaving the hostel at one, and I didn't think we'd be back in time. So we're going to drive back, just the three of us. Okay?"

Three? I turned around to see Bayne in the back seat, breathing heavily, as if he'd been running.

"How are you feeling?" Jordan asked.

How was I feeling? I was numb. I felt nothing.

"I'm all right. I didn't get to talk to her at all, you know. She was shot just after she got out of the car."

Jordan nodded. "It doesn't matter. She can't hurt anyone now. Not you, not the United States of America, not the world."

"But *I* didn't save the world," I said.

"You helped," he replied. "You got her out here."

I digested his words slowly. I was still in a state of shock; I could have been misinterpreting them.

"Do you think the killer knew she was meeting me?" A sensation I couldn't identify crept up on me. Not sad, no way. But I wasn't so numb anymore. I wasn't sure if this was a good thing, because I didn't particularly want any feelings to return.

Jordan took his eyes off the road just long enough to glance at me. "He's probably been following her," he said.

"Then I had nothing to do with it," I said. "He would have killed her anywhere."

"Right."

The voice from the back seat piped up. "Who cares?"

"What did you say?"

"Who cares?" Bayne repeated. "She's dead, that's what matters. Hey, remember *The Wizard of Oz*? 'Ding-dong the witch is dead.' We should be celebrating."

"Bayne," Jordan said, in a warning voice.

Bayne just shrugged. I guessed I couldn't blame him for being so . . . so callous. He didn't know the whole story.

Jordan reached out to the dashboard and turned on the radio.

". . . and police are scouring the area, searching for clues that might lead them to the killer. It happened at precisely noon, on a quiet suburban street just east of the District of Columbia. It is unknown what Senator Hunsucker was doing on the street at that hour. Her staff has—"

Jordan changed the channel. Now the car was filled with something classical. He glanced at me again.

"I'm okay," I said, though not very convincingly.

He shook his head. "I don't care what you say, you've got to be freaked out. Why don't you close your eyes and try to get some sleep." He turned down the music.

Obediently, I closed my eyes. My mind was replaying the song Jordan had brought up. "Ding-dong the witch is dead. Which old witch? The wicked witch." Funny, I hadn't watched the movie for years, but I could still remember most of the words. "She's gone where the goblins go, below. . . ." Was that where she was now? Surely not anywhere near my place. The truly, horribly wicked people didn't end up in my neighborhood. Even though she hadn't had the opportunity to carry out her terrible plans, the intentions had to count for something. Maybe right this very minute she was being welcomed by Satan himself.

"Ding-dong the witch is dead." I visualized the scene from the movie. All those little Munchkins, dancing around Dorothy and her little dog, Toto. They were celebrating. I didn't feel like celebrating. I didn't know what I was feeling. So, as usual, sleep became my way to escape.

"Hey, Sleeping Beauty."

I opened my eyes. We were off the highway now, and I recognized the area. Woodbridge was just off this road. "How long did I sleep?"

"About an hour and a half. How are you feeling?"

"Okay," I lied. Apparently, Bayne had been in need of sleep, too. From the back seat came the sound of snoring, which was preferable to hearing him sing. "Where are we going now?"

"I've gotta find you a place to stay. There's a nice inn not far from St. Andrews; my parents stay there when they come to visit me."

But there was no room at the inn. Jordan drove back to the highway. We spotted a big vacancy sign outside a motel, and he pulled into it. It didn't look disgusting, but it wasn't exactly homey.

"I hate to leave you here," he said.

"Can't you stay with me?"

"No, I have to get back to the dorm. We're only allowed to disappear for a certain amount of time and then they start calling parents." He came into the reception office with me, paid for a night in advance, and walked me to the room. It wasn't too bad, just sort of bland and characterless. If there was a motel in one of the better neighborhoods of Hell, it would look like this. I almost smiled.

"This is just for tonight," Jordan assured me. "Tomorrow I'll find something nicer for you. Are you hungry? The man at the desk said there's a coffee shop." He took out his wallet and put some bills on the dresser.

"Maybe later," I said. "You go on, get back to school. And, Jordan . . ."

"What?"

I hesitated. "Nothing, never mind."

It wasn't nothing, of course. I just couldn't bring myself to come right out and demand to know if I'd been used to set my mother up. We kissed, and he was gone.

I had a long bath. Then I considered going to the coffee shop, but instead I went to the row of snack machines just outside my door, loaded up on chips and candy bars, and went back to the room. The motel had cable, and I found a movie channel that didn't have any news. To this day, I couldn't tell you what movies I watched that night. But I just watched one after another, until I fell asleep again.

The set was still on when I woke up the next morning. I'd had a good long sleep, without any disturbing dreams (that I could remember), but I still wasn't feeling particularly energetic. I managed to brush my teeth and get dressed, and I was once again contemplating the coffee shop when there was a knock on my door.

It was Jordan. He gave me a hug. "I really hated leaving you last night. Did you get any sleep?"

I searched his face, and all I saw was exhaustion and concern. This was not the face of someone who had anything to do with murder, I told myself. We left the room, pausing outside before a newspaper vending machine. The headline held no surprise for me, though it was still something of a shock to see the unusually large print.

HUNSUCKER ASSASSINATED

"What's the difference between murder and assassination?" I wondered out loud.

"I guess you have to be really important to be considered assassinated instead of just murdered or killed." He dropped a coin in the slot and took out a paper. Once we were in the car, I opened it.

There were a lot of photos of my mother inside, taken at various points in her illustrious career. There was one I'd never seen before. The caption read: "The birth of Margaret Hunsucker's only child, the late Jessica Hunsucker, shortly after the death of Harley Hunsucker." The sixteen-year-old photo showed my mother beaming tenderly at the baby in her arms.

"I'll bet she tossed you to the nanny two seconds after the cameras flashed," Jordan commented.

"You're probably right. Where are we going? To the inn?"

"Better. The assistant headmaster and his family have an apartment attached to the residence hall. Their kid's away on a school trip for a week, so they're going to let you have his room."

"How did you explain me to them?"

"I just told them you were my girlfriend and you'd come to visit. Oh, and I said you were eighteen, so they won't bother you about why aren't you in school and where are your parents. It's not going to be an issue, Matt Kelly is cool, and so is his wife. I bet I'll even be able to stay with you."

"That'll be good," I said with a lot of feeling in my voice. Maybe too much feeling.

"Of course, I can't be with you all the time," he cautioned. "I have classes."

"Oh, that's okay," I said quickly. "I understand. You say I can stay there for a week?"

"Yep. You'll just need to lay low, so other kids don't get the idea they can all set their girls up there. And by the end of the week, I'll have something else figured out for you."

Should I tell him that wouldn't be necessary? For all

intents and purposes, my mission on earth was finished. Brad could come for me anytime.

But he didn't come that day. Jordan introduced me to the assistant headmaster and his wife, and, like he said, they were cool. He was the type who liked to be thought of as a pal to the students, and Heather, his wife, was easygoing. I had their ten-year-old son's room, decorated with football and X-Men posters, and the run of the whole apartment. Just moments after I arrived, Mr. Kelly went to a meeting and Mrs. Kelly had a lunch date, so Jordan and I had the place to ourselves.

"Do you have a class now?" I asked.

"Yeah," he said, "but I haven't cut it in a while. And I'd rather be with you." So we ended up squeezed together in the son's single bed.

It was nice, feeling his arms around me, but I wasn't really into it, and Jordan could tell. "What's wrong?"

"I don't know. It's not you. I guess I'm just still in a weird mood after what happened yesterday. I'm not feeling very sexy."

He was sweet about it. Before he went to his next class, we made cappuccinos in the Kellys' fancy machine and sat together at the kitchen table. The family's newspaper was sitting there. I turned it over so I wouldn't have to look at the headline.

"Too bad we have to keep your identity a secret," Jordan mused. "It would make a great news story. You'd be famous! I could see you now, on *60 Minutes* or *Letterman*."

I gave him a reproving look. "Like anyone would believe it? I can see it now. 'Our special guest tonight—Jessica Hunsucker, sold by her mother to the devil, will share her stories of life in Hell!'"

"I'm not talking about that," Jordan said. "I'm thinking more along the lines of a daughter's selfless act." He was watching me carefully now, and waiting for my response.

I guess I'd known all along, but it still wasn't easy getting the words out. "You planned this, didn't you? You got me to contact Lisa and set up this meeting with my mother so you'd know exactly where she would be. Did you shoot her?"

He shook his head.

"Was it Bayne?"

"It doesn't matter now," he said. "What's done is done." He took my hand. "I know what you're thinking, that I just used you to get your mother. It's not true, Jessica. I care about you, a lot."

"Then why couldn't you tell me what you were planning?"

"Because I knew you wouldn't go along with it if you knew she'd be killed. You wouldn't have, would you?"

"No."

"Don't hate me, Jessica," he said. "It was the only way."

"I don't hate you," I replied, and I was pretty sure that was the truth.

He left soon after that. I tried to keep busy, mainly by reading. The Kelly family had a lot of books. I'd missed reading so much in Hell, I'd thought that if I was ever around good books again I could just read and read forever. But after a few hours, I realized books were like any good thing—too much was too much. You could actually get tired of it, like chocolate.

Thinking of chocolate made me think of that crazy lady at the secondhand shop in Hell. I wondered what *she* had done to get there. I thought back to how annoyed I'd been, to find myself in Hell when I hadn't done anything wrong. At least now, maybe I'd feel like I deserved to be there. I'd played a part in a murder. I could tell myself that I was innocent, that I didn't know this could happen, but was that really true? I knew how committed Jordan was, how determined he was to stop Margaret Hunsucker. I could have predicted this.

I wondered if Brad was watching right now, and what he thought about it. What he thought about me. Was he shocked by what had happened? By what I'd done?

It was a long day. Heather Kelly came back and asked me if I wanted to go with her to get a manicure, but it seemed like a kind of frivolous thing to be doing only twenty-four hours after aiding in the murder of your mother. So I stayed in the bedroom, read the son's comic books, and waited for Jordan.

He came back around five, and I was glad to see him. All I wanted to do was curl up with him, not for sex this time, just to talk, to spill out all these conflicted feelings and let him comfort me. But Jordan had other plans.

"The gang's getting together over at Dobbs. Some girls from Woodbridge are coming, Bayne's sneaking in a keg of beer, a couple of guys are picking up buckets at KFC, and I've got an excellent playlist on my PC. C'mon, we both need this."

"Need what? A celebration?"

"*No.* Just some rest and relaxation. Jessica, babe, I know how you must be feeling. But you didn't do anything wrong, and brooding over it isn't going to make things any better."

"I did nothing wrong," I repeated. "Jordan, my mother is dead. And I helped get her killed."

"And are you going to tell me now that you're in mourning for her? That you're sad and you miss her and you wish she was here with you right now?"

"No . . . but I don't feel good about it."

He sighed. "Jessica, listen to me. Yes, Margaret Hunsucker is dead. An evil woman who wanted to destroy the world as we know it will not have a chance to do it. Is that such a terrible thing?"

I didn't answer.

He went on. "Did you know there was this group of Germans during World War II who tried to assassinate Adolf

Hitler? They didn't pull it off—the bomb they planted didn't kill Hitler—but if it had worked, do you think those guys would have felt guilty? Do you know how many lives might have been saved?" He smiled. "And I'll bet those guys would have been partying that night. I can see them all right now, at the beer garden, singing, 'Ding-dong the Nazi's dead!'"

I considered this. "Were any of those guys Hitler's son?"

"I don't think Hitler had any children. But you know what? He had a nephew. And that nephew moved to the United States and joined the military. So he had something to do with bringing down his own uncle. He played a part in saving the world. Just like you did."

He was right. He just didn't understand. But, then, neither did I.

So we went over to the Dobbs Commons. Almost all the kids from the demonstration trip were there, plus a bunch of girls from Woodbridge. Some of them I recognized, others were strangers, but it didn't matter, since none of them knew me. As usual, Jordan was immediately surrounded. I backed away, accepted a beer, and stood against the wall.

Everything Jordan had said to me was true. I hated her, she hated me, she had evil intentions, and we were all better off now that she was dead. But there was still this one thing. Whatever else she was . . . she'd given birth to me. Which meant she was my mother, even if she never acted like one, even if I never felt like a daughter. And that was why this was going to be on my mind, or at least in the back of my mind, forever. I had to make Jordan understand.

I looked for him, and saw him talking to a girl. He caught my eye and waved me over to join them.

"Janie, this is Amanda," he said.

I recognized her—a large, sporty-looking girl with a friendly face. She was student-body president at Woodbridge.

"You won't believe what Amanda just told me," Jordan went on. "Tell her, Amanda."

"This is so awful," Amanda reported. "Yesterday, in Richmond, this pregnant woman started having labor pains on the street. Some couple saw her, and they put her in their car and took her to the closest hospital. But the hospital wouldn't let her in because she didn't have insurance. She had the baby in the parking lot! The couple stayed with her and tried to help, they got the baby out, but the woman died. They're trying to keep it hushed up, but I know someone who knows someone who works at the hospital."

"We've got to get the media on to this," Jordan said. "I've got the name of a guy over at Channel Six."

"It's absolutely disgraceful, the health-care system in this country," Amanda declared. "This kind of thing would never happen in England or France. It shouldn't be happening here."

"Let's do something," Jordan suggested. "Let's organize a march on the hospital, get some attention. You in on this with us, Jess—Janie?"

"Sure," I said. I didn't know much about the health-care system, but I'd heard there were a lot of problems, and if someone could die because she didn't have insurance, that wasn't right. So Jordan was finished with Margaret Hunsucker and on to the next cause.

When we left, he was still talking about hospitals and health care. I nodded and agreed, but I didn't say much, and I guess I wasn't as enthusiastic as he wanted me to be. We'd reached the door to the Kelly apartment when he asked, "You're still thinking about your mother, aren't you?"

It was on the tip of my tongue to say, No, I'm thinking about people who don't have medical insurance, and I did care about that, really I did, but there was something else I cared about, too, that was taking precedent.

"Yes and no," I said.

"Jess. . . ." He sounded tired.

"No, wait, listen to me," I said. I had an idea, an example that might help him to understand my mixed-up feelings. "It's not so weird that I'm a little depressed. Haven't you ever heard about adopted people who are perfectly happy with the parents who raised them, who love them very much, but still feel this need to find their birth mother? And even if that birth mother turns out to be someone who didn't care about giving up her baby, and hadn't had one thought about the son or daughter since, and didn't even want to meet him or her now—the adopted person still wants to see the birth mother. There's a *connection*, can you see that? Even if there's no love, there's a connection!"

He looked at me in disbelief. "Are you telling me you felt connected to your mother? The woman who sent you to Hell?"

"I don't *know*! I'm just saying I don't feel right."

Jordan sighed, and ran his fingers through his hair. "I don't know what to say."

And then I knew why. Because he would never be able to understand. Not because he was insensitive, or uncaring. But because . . .

You know how there are people who can't see the forest for the trees? They can't see the big picture, they only look at the little things. Jordan sees the forest just fine. What he can't see are the individual trees.

I was a tree.

Jordan cared about people, society, the world. But at that moment in time, I needed someone to care about me, just me. And in the following moment, I knew what I had to do.

"Don't mind me, I'm just tired," I lied.

He looked almost relieved. "Yeah, me, too. I guess I'll head back to my room."

I nodded. Then we kissed. I wish I could say it was terribly poignant and full of unspoken feelings and it left an imprint on my heart, but really it was just a kiss.

For the zillionth time over the past couple of days, I wondered if Brad was watching. And I wondered what he'd say about all this. I imagined myself talking to him: Brad, I helped kill my mother. Was it bad, what I did? Am I stupid to feel the way I'm feeling now? You know about these things, you've had experiences. . . . Tell me what to do now, tell me what to do with these feelings.

I didn't even undress. I lay back on the bed with my eyes open, staring at the ceiling, and fell into a fitful sleep.

This time I *did* have dreams. I was back in my mother's house, the Hunsucker homestead, in my bedroom. Brad came to me. He seemed real and unreal, just like when I first saw him. The only difference was that I wasn't afraid this time, because I knew why he was there.

"You've come to take me away."

He didn't respond. I thought his eyes were sad.

"She's dead, you know," I said.

He spoke. "I know. I saw it."

Then I knew I wasn't in my mother's house, and I wasn't dreaming. I sat up.

"Were you watching all the time I was here, Brad?"

"No, not all the time. Not when you didn't want me to watch."

But he knew what had happened between me and Jordan. I could tell. "Are you angry?"

"No."

Even in that tiny one-syllable word, I heard something I didn't believe.

"You've got a right to be angry," I continued. "I'm your mate."

He shrugged. "In Hell. You're on earth now."

"But I still belong to you."

He made a face. "I really hate that expression," he said. "Okay, yeah, according to Satan, you belong to me. But . . . but that doesn't mean you have to love me."

There was a moment of silence.

"Brad, did you ever love anyone?"

"I'm not sure. Do you love Jordan?"

"I'm not sure," I echoed. Did I love Jordan? Strange how I hadn't been agonizing over *those* feelings at all.

There was another silence.

"Brad . . . am I crazy? I can't stop thinking about my mother. I came here to stop her, and she's been stopped, but I feel . . . well, not happy."

"You're entitled to feel weird," he said. "As awful as she was, she was still your mother. And you did have something to do with the fact that she's dead now, so you have to feel a little guilty."

That was the word. *Guilty.* "You get it, don't you? How I feel."

"Sure, I get it. It's only human." There was a flicker of a smile on his face. "That's funny, huh? Maybe you have to be a demon to understand what's human."

"You're still human," I said.

I wasn't sure if he heard me. "Look, Jessica, you didn't luck out as far as parents go. You had a racist redneck for a father and a fascist tyrant for a mother. But, hey, they *made* you. You wouldn't exist if it wasn't for them. And especially her—you came out of her body. There's a connection. How could you feel nothing?"

"I feel bad," I whispered. "I'm not sorry she's dead, but I feel bad. You understand that, don't you." It was a statement, not a question. But I had a question, too. "Does this make sense?"

"Of course it makes sense. Good people don't kill other people. Not even bad people. You feel bad because you're good." He scratched his head. "I'm not saying this very well."

"I get it," I said. "It's like how you felt when those people in the hospital died. You felt bad because you're good."

There it was, that crooked little anxious smile. "Yeah, well, don't spread it around. I've got a pretty cushy deal going for me down in you-know-where, and I don't want to lose my job."

My heart was full. "I won't tell anyone, Brad. Your secret is safe with me."

"Thanks." He paused. "Listen, I've got something else to tell you."

"What's that?"

"You don't have to come back. To Hell. With me."

I stared at him. "I don't understand."

"I can pull some strings," he said. "A big shot I know owes me a favor. You can stay here, with Jordan."

I was too stunned to speak. "Are you serious?"

"I know how you feel about him," Brad said. "Don't worry, I didn't *watch*," he added hastily. "But I could see how you looked at him." He paused. "He seems like a good person."

"He is good," I admitted. "He wants justice, and fairness. He wants the world to be a better place, and he's willing to work hard to make it that way. He sees the big picture. The forest."

"Whatever," Brad said. "All I'm saying is, you can stay on earth. I can't help you out with identity papers or anything like that, you'll be on your own, but you can live out a normal life span. You can grow up, you can have kids. With Jordan, if that's what you want." He fumbled in his pocket. "I've got something here for you to sign. . . ."

"Do I have to stay?"

He looked up. "What?"

I didn't really have to repeat what I'd asked. He'd heard me perfectly well, I could see it in his eyes.

At that moment in time, all his attention was on me, all his senses were attuned to me. I reached out and took his hand.

"Brad, let's go home."

EPILOGUE

I'VE WRITTEN a story with a beginning, a middle, and an end. But if you're like me, you always want to know what happened after the end, so I'm going to add a little.

In regular earth time, all that I've written took place almost a year ago. Life on earth is nowhere near perfect, but it's in no worse shape than it was before Margaret Hunsucker. There's a president who does some good things and makes some mistakes but has generally decent intentions.

Brad and I are a real couple now, with all that word implies. We're still in the same house, and it looks pretty much the same, except I did take down those tacky pictures, the big-eyed kids and the dogs playing cards. There's not much else I can do about the décor.

Brad's still a demon, of course, and he's still working in basic temptations, but he's up for promotion. He thinks he wants to become a collector, going to earth to pick up people who sold their own souls to the devil.

I still don't have a job, but I'm keeping busy. Brad and I worked together on figuring out a method to photograph books on TV while people were reading them. It takes a long time, and I wish I could locate some speed-readers on earth. Still, slowly but surely, we're building up a real book collection, and I've started lending books out. I'm even thinking about starting up a real library. There's no actual law that says we can't have one in Hell, mainly because the power structure can't imagine there are people who would think of libraries as fun places. Just like they can't imagine anyone enjoying a Big Mac.

Remember how I wanted to study Italian? I found out that there are more French people here than Italians, so I found a university French course on TV that I've been following. Sometimes I have French people over here for conversation. We have canned baked beans and hot dogs with Hawaiian Punch for dinner, and pretend it's cassoulet with red wine.

I've learned to be more creative, too. Back on earth, I always loved playing Scrabble, even by myself. Now I've made my own game, with letters I cut out of the newspapers and magazines that Brad smuggles home. And Brad's trying to catch up on the new technologies. He wants to figure out how we can access museums directly, and be able to see all the artwork from different perspectives. We're talking about trying to print out copies of some paintings and enlarging them, so we can have something over the sofa to replace the card-playing dogs.

Brad's even helped me check on Jordan a couple of times. I must admit, I was gratified to see how dismayed he was over my disappearance, but he recovered pretty quickly. He's gotten heavily involved with ecological causes, and he's got a new girlfriend—not Ashley, thank goodness.

Angie next door recently got me involved in a neighborhood group. We've had an influx of suicide bombers recently, and they're having a hard time here. This was not where they'd expected to end up, so they're super pissed-off, and they're not adjusting well at all. My group is working on integrating them into the community.

And we're petitioning for a bowling alley. It's the kind of sport that real athletes look down on, so, based on the rationale for our fast-food restaurants, we just might have a solid crack at getting one.

I'm not trying to make this place sound like paradise. It's still Hell. I miss good food, I miss Starbucks—we never did get one down here. I miss the Gap. Our homemade stapled books don't feel as nice in your hands as real books. I tried gardening, so we could have some fresh vegetables to eat, but that didn't work. Because the soil isn't real, it doesn't have the right minerals for growing stuff.

But life—or death—could be a lot worse. It's amazing how little you really need, and how you can learn to make do with what you have. And I've got Brad. He's my lover and my best friend, we can talk to each other about everything, and we never run out of subjects. Which is a good thing, since we're going to be spending a long, long time together.